Rescue Me
When God Says Yes

CHERYL BARTON

Published by: Cheryl Barton Publishing, LLC

Cheryl Barton Publishing, LLC
P.O. Box 962
Reisterstown, Maryland 21136
www.crbarton.com
or
Email: prez@crbarton.com

Ordering Information:
Quantity sales.
Special discounts are available on quantity purchases by corporations, associations, and others. For details, contact the publisher at the address above.

Orders by U.S. trade bookstores and wholesalers.
Please contact prez@crbarton.com

ISBN: 1-948950-69-3
ISBN-13: 978-1-948950-69-5

About "Rescue Me"

Marissa Ballard is "Delilah" living a life of shame in the eyes of her family and finally, herself. She's lost faith, not believing in a way out of her current circumstance. She tried living according to rules that weren't meant for her because her immediate desires outweighed the vision of what her life could be if she had stayed faithful.

One day, Marissa was so far down in the dumps over where life had taken her that she hated who she had become, a woman who turned her back on her parents and her six-year-old daughter, Lacey, for a life with a man who demeaned and degraded her. Shame kept her from going back to her life in Philadelphia, instead opting to let a man use her for his own selfish desires, tricking her into believing what she felt from him was love. Finally, sick and tired of being sick and tired, she called out to the only help she remembered her parents telling her she should call on when she was in need, but even then, she didn't pause long enough to listen and know that her cry had been heard and her path to redemption was being newly paved.

Roman Hale spent a lifetime rescuing those in distress, but couldn't save the one woman who was the light of his life, his dying wife. His heart was about to give up on a life of service until the revelation of a new purpose and a new love shocked him into belief. Roman wasn't sure his heart was as open as it once was and just when he thought about giving up on being that lifeline to the less fortunate, his eyes were opened to the reality that one great love in life would not be his only love.

Marissa didn't know that her cry for help would lead her on a path that collided with Philadelphia Police Officer, Roman Hale. Together they will discover the love they both wanted, needed and deserved because the foundation is just right.

Acknowledgement

What do you believe God can do for you? Are you a believer that He can rescue you from every situation? You can never sink too low that he can't pull you up out of your mess. You are never too far away that He can't pull you back into His loving arms if you're open to what He desires for you. He will love the person you see in the mirror that you're not happy with. He can and will rescue you from those things that keep you from your destiny.

Maybe you don't hear His voice, perhaps you don't feel His love, but He will show up, sometimes in forms that are not obvious. Know that He's there and all you have to do is open your eyes, open your heart and believe that your rescue is right in front of you. Let go and let God and then believe that *HE WILL!*

Thank you for believing that faith can heal your heart and break a pattern of self-destruct that can lead you to the love of your life!

1

Roman Hale's heart was hurting while his mind raced a million miles a minute wondering if there was some transgression in his past that caused karma to pay him a visit and attack his life at its very core. The life he'd prayed for and thought would last an eternity was supposed to consist of happy smiles and happy times each and every day, yet here he was facing the biggest challenge of his life. He had to find a way to hold on even though the inevitable was staring him in the face.

The dilemma before him had to be a result of something he'd done that he was being punished for because the angelic woman laying before him, hooked up to machines and sleeping peacefully due to the medication seeping through her veins didn't deserve to have her life cut short. His Melanie, oh his Melanie, his greatest love was dying and his faith was being tested.

She was beautiful, young and vibrant and should be up moving about with the zest for life she'd had since the day he'd met her. She deserved a life filled with many more early mornings and late nights, holding hands with him and planning for the many family vacations they'd talked about for years. The reality was, that wasn't meant to be. Melanie was in the fight for her own life and he didn't know what else to do. He wasn't sure he was prepared for what was next.

Pacing nervously, Roman barely heard the usual thud his bare feet made when he walked across the soft, plush platinum colored, glam shag carpet that covered the floor of the bedroom he shared with Melanie. He smiled briefly remembering the day she'd forced him to remove his shoes and socks to feel the carpet under his feet. She wanted him to enjoy the little things in life like she did and he'd never forget how excited new carpet made her. He told her being in love with carpet was a woman thing, but still, he relented and did as she asked. He admitted, he loved the carpet and now realized how trivial the argument had been back then over whether to get the very expensive carpet or keep the hardwood floors.

Today, he moved almost in stealth mode with his footsteps being cat-like as he tried not to disturb her serene posture as she slept peacefully. He looked down at his feet knowing he would normally wear socks on his feet, but Melanie told him that while she was bedridden, she loved the feel of his bare feet rubbing against her bare legs. No request from Melanie was too great and so he would perform that husbandly duty even if she wasn't as alert to his presence as she had once been.

Melanie loved to feel him close to her, though there were times when she was barely conscious enough to know that he was there. As she slept, he wafted back and forth at the foot of their cherry queen poster bed, waiting for the home health nurse, Hannah, to finish taking Melanie's vitals and making sure the pain medication was doing the job of allowing her to rest without discomfort. He could see the rise and fall of her steady breathing under the soft navy blue down comforter that covered the bed. Seeing it brought back another memory of the day he'd gone shopping with her for new bedding on the very day he had surprised her with a new bedroom set for their last anniversary. Without his input, she had already decided to redecorate the room in the same shades of blue that the wedding party wore at their wedding some years ago. Time was moving too fast and tender moments like their wedding day were overshadowed by Melanie's declining health. His number one priority was making sure she knew how much she was loved.

He'd gotten up earlier in the morning to tend to their one-year-old daughter, Nina, who was now napping in the adjourning bedroom. Roman found himself conformed to her schedule and once he had her down, he'd been able to grab a shower, change into clean sweat pants and a t-shirt and as soon as the nurse was finished, he was planning on getting back in the bed to cuddle up close to Melanie. For the past two weeks, that had been his morning routine and thanks to a police captain who told him to take as much time as he needed with his family, he didn't have to stress over time at home or time on the job as a policeman for the Philadelphia police department.

As he watched her sleeping, something seemed different. Melanie's breathing was shallow, much more than usual and she hadn't been as alert as she had been on previous days. He didn't physically smell it, but he had a feeling the smell of death was invading their space and he didn't like it as he tried to push the mere thought out of his head. He tried to prepare himself like others told him he should, but it was hard. She was his love, his life. Medicine hadn't work, prayer didn't appear to be working and though he prayed not just for Melanie to survive the illness, but also, if there was no way for her to ever get out of that bed again and hold their precious daughter, he didn't want her to be in any pain. That prayer had been answered. He hated thinking about the fact that the other prayer, which would require more, wasn't going to be answered. There was no doubt the words he had been dreading hearing were on the tip of the nurse's tongue as she looked to him and then back to Melanie. Each time she looked his way, he caught her glimpse before she would dart her eyes in another direction, avoiding eye contact as she contemplated how to give him the heart wrenching news. He held his breath as she removed the stethoscope from her ears, exhaled and then with a solemn look on her face, addressed him.

"I'm sorry Roman, but I think the time is near and you should prepare yourself to say goodbye as the doctor confirmed for you earlier. Melanie isn't in any pain, as you requested and we've made her as comfortable as we can. Doctor Edwards will be back in shortly after finishing up a call he had to take and he'll share with you what you can expect over the next several hours. Is there anything we can do for you at this time?" Hannah asked softly. He appreciated, not only the care she gave to Melanie, but also the comforting tone in how she addressed him.

Roman held his breath as he listened while preparing his already rapidly beating heart to hear the words he dreaded. After months of fighting a disease with no cure, the love of his life would soon be gone. Hannah had been Melanie's nurse since the moment she came home from the hospital after having Nina. Things occurred in a blur from the moment they'd heard the word cancer.

It had been detected while Melanie had been pregnant with Nina and there was never a question of whether she would continue with the pregnancy despite her medical condition. Together in their faith, they believed that whatever happened would be the will of God. He was ecstatic the day she'd told him she was pregnant and then during her checkup at the end of her first trimester, the cancer had been discovered in her breasts. Though there was no immediate danger to the baby, without treatment, they were told that Melanie would not survive and that they could lose her and or the baby. They prayed and decided their baby deserved a chance.

After giving birth, her doctors aggressively treated the cancer which they found had already advanced and there wasn't a lot they could do with the cancer growing at an expeditious rate. Eventually, Nina had been born happy and healthy and now he had to deal with living his life without his wife as he raised their daughter alone, without her.

Roman tried to speak, but the words were lodged in his throat as he fought back tears. This was not the way life was supposed to be. At twenty-six, he thought life would be different, but here he was trying to come up with the words to say goodbye.

Overwhelmed with emotions, he held his breath as he turned and exited the bedroom to get himself together. He needed Melanie to see him strong or she would fight leaving him and Nina if she knew they weren't ready for her departure from this life. Even after stepping outside of the room and closing the door behind him, he was still afraid to let go for fear that he wouldn't be able to control the tears he knew were already falling from his eyes or the spasms his body would go through knowing the woman he vowed to love, honor and cherish would soon be taking her last breath. He wasn't ready even though he knew this day was coming. What was he going to do? What would he and Nina do without her? He stood outside of the closed door wiping away the tears and inhaled deeply before reaching for the doorknob to go back in, not wanting to miss even a moment with the love of his life. Taking one last large deep breath, he re-entered the bedroom and smiled at Hannah.

"Sorry about that," he explained.

"No need to apologize. I understand and it's okay. Are you sure there isn't anything I can do for you or get you?" she asked again.

"No, thank you, there isn't anything else you can do at this time. You and your team have been wonderful to my wife and I appreciate all you've done. I'm going to sit with her just in case she can feel my presence. I want to talk to her so that she can hear my voice as God calls her home," he said. Though the pain was deep, he held himself together for her.

"Very well, sir. I'll leave you to your quiet time with your wife. Ring me if you need anything," she said.

Roman nodded and watched as Hannan left the bedroom. He walked closer to the bed as the sight of Melanie, who was now a mere shell of the vibrant woman she once was, consumed him. She had lost a lot of weight as the cancer that had ravaged her body took everything from her, but what remained was the beauty he had fallen in love with. For him, nothing could ever take that away.

Roman's mind went back to the day they stood before God and their families and pledged their lives to each other, a pledge that meant forever to them. Throughout his life, he'd been taught to believe in God and His plan for his life. Through the trials of Melanie's cancer diagnosis and failed treatment, he still trusted and believed that God was in control and that Melanie would be okay – she had to be. Isn't that what prayer and faith were about? Then came the day when modern medicine could no longer sustain her. What he was going through was causing an inner struggle with his faith.

Nothing could have prepared him for what was ahead. Walking over to the bed as the doctor walked into the room toward him, Roman smiled and took his hand in his and thanked him for all he'd done. He was thankful that he was able to have Melanie in the comfort of their home at the end, a place he knew she would want to be. He watched as the doctor checked a few of the machines that were connected to her, looked at the notes the nurse had written down and then after a quick check of Melanie, there were no words needed. The expression on the doctor's face said everything. If there was a change, the doctor would have said so, but instead, he turned and left the room, leaving him to his time with her.

Roman gently slid onto the bed and moved as close as he could to Melanie, placing his head next to hers to be sure she could feel that he was right with her.

"Baby, I know you probably can't hear me, but I hope you can feel my presence. Nina and I love you and we already miss you. I said a prayer that if God wasn't going to heal you of this, that He would be gracious and remove any pain so that you no longer suffered. I want you to know I'm here with you and I will be until God says it's your time. I don't know how to handle this, but I'm trying. I'm really trying to hold on to my faith, but this is hard. This is a struggle and normally, you would give me some words to live by and to encourage me to see the brighter side of any situation that tests me. Who's going to do that when you're gone? I love you. I love you so much and I'm sorry that I'm letting you down by questioning God right now. You would never settle for that, instead telling me that God has a reason for everything He allows to happen, but this, I'm having a hard time with. I asked God to heal you and He didn't say yes. I asked Him to give me and Nina more years with you and He didn't say yes. I believe in Him, I trust Him and I'm sorry to say that I don't understand Him right now."

Roman inhaled deeply and as he exhaled, he moved even closer to Melanie so that he could wrap his arm across her body while planting soft kisses on her cheek.

"I'm sorry, baby. I'm sorry I couldn't do anything to help you heal. I'm sorry that maybe my faith wasn't strong enough and my words and pleas didn't reach God's ears. I'm going to miss you like crazy. I promise to make sure that Nina will always know how much you loved her and how much you wanted to be here with her, but that wasn't to be. Know that my love for you will never die. I love you."

Taking Melanie's hand in his, Roman cried himself to sleep knowing that soon, he'd be without her and deep in his heart, he was questioning God's no.

2

"Hello? Hello?" the voice said.

Marissa Ballard started to say something, but the words wouldn't come out. Her head was pounding with the same worry she'd had for the past hour as she contemplated making the call she didn't think would amount to much. She thought that any second, the phone would slip from her nervously shaken, twitching fingers. She'd been rubbing them so vigorously to the point that they were numb.

Marissa looked around, checking her surroundings in the unfamiliar territory. She had driven quite a distance to find a pay phone and yet again, she couldn't form words knowing if she didn't find any, the call would disconnect as it had so many times in the past year. Just as she was about to return the greeting, the call ended.

"Ugh," she said frustrated with herself. She looked around to see if anyone watched her nervously tapping on the wall beside the phone and hoped she wouldn't be asked to leave before she called again. It wasn't easy paying the right person to get inside of the occupied high school to make the call. Luckily a parent took pity on her and helped her out. After all, even at twenty-one, she could actually pass for one of the students at the school due to her youthful look. With security as tight as it was these days, she was surprised it was as easy as it was to get inside to use the phone. There was no way she could use her own cell phone knowing that no one on the other end would even attempt to answer if they saw it was her who was calling. Well, maybe her father would, but her mother, not in this lifetime.

Reaching for more change in the pocket of her tight designer jeans, she slid the coins in the slot, dialed the number again and waited. This time, she would find the strength.

"Hello?" the voice asked again.

Marissa opened her mouth, but no words again came out.

"Hello? Is someone there? If you're there and speaking, I can't hear you," the deep voice said.

Clearing her throat, Marissa's eyes widened knowing she'd been heard. She couldn't remain silent now or the next time, the caller wouldn't answer.

"Yyyyesss," she stuttered out and then there was a pause.

"Marissa? Marissa, is that you? Are you there?"

She took in a large gulp of air and tried her best to stand strong. At least it wasn't her mother.

"Yes, daddy. It's me. I'm sorry for the first call. I

couldn't get the words out," she explained.

"I thought it was you, but I wasn't sure. You've been doing this a lot, calling and not saying anything. Is everything okay? How are you?" he asked.

Marissa smiled when her father's voice softened.

"I'm doing okay. How is Lacey?" she asked.

"Your daughter is fine and could use her mother in her life. A one-year-old little girl needs her mother," William Ballard declared.

As images of her daughter laughing and playing raced through her mind, she felt deflated. She wasn't a mother in any true sense of the word other than the fact that she'd given birth. She had dropped Lacey off in Philadelphia with her parents after one month of giving birth and then turned her back on that life to follow one she thought she wanted and now knew that she'd made a terrible mistake. She couldn't think of a way back to her old life after the embarrassment and shame she knew greeted her every time she thought about facing her parents again. She'd left home at eighteen with no money and no real plan for her life other than to find what she thought would be a better one than the one she lived at home. That didn't happen and she struggled with what direction to go in.

"She doesn't need a woman like me. She deserves much better than me, daddy," she grumbled.

"Don't do that, Marissa. Don't you ever call me and downplay the woman I know you can be despite who you have become. I raised you and I know what you're capable of. The problem is you don't know the woman you were created to be and that isn't a woman who leaves her baby and barely looks back other than a few phone calls here and there and boxes of toys and clothes sent in the mail. Lacey deserves more than that," he said.

"I'm so ashamed," she admitted.

"Then do something about it so that you're not. The only person standing in your way is you and well, that man, that gangster who will remain nameless right now. You still have the power to make a change. You have the power to choose that life or one that includes your daughter. You're missing so much with her. She started walking right before her birthday."

Marissa perked up, grinning from ear to ear. She imagined Lacey's little legs taking their first steps and how proud she felt knowing she was being taken care of. Still, she was missing it all.

"Really? I bet she's into everything. Did you get the presents I sent last week?" she asked. "I wanted her to have them in time for her birthday," she added.

Marissa thought about the trunk load of toys for a one-year-old little girl that she'd gone to the post office to mail to her parents the week before Lacey's first birthday. She had no doubt her parents had gone all out for a party and she only wished she had the nerve to show up in Philadelphia.

"Yes, and you almost caused a fight between your mother and me. She didn't want to give them to Lacey and you know I did. Everything was so nice and I finally had to make an actual play room out of the other bedroom. Between what you bought, the things your mother and I bought and the presents from family, friends and people at church, that baby could open her own toy and clothing store. We gave some away to needy families."

Marissa could hear her father smiling through the phone.

"Somehow, I knew you would," she replied.

Marissa smiled at the happiness she heard in his voice though she knew their relationship was strained. He father still spoke with her in a joyful voice, but her mother was another story. She still refused to even talk to her when she called home.

"She'll never forgive me, will she? She'll always be ashamed of me, won't she?" she asked thinking about how hardened her mother's heart had turned toward her.

Marissa knew that she could count on her father to not make her feel ashamed. Her mother thrived on putting her down. They hadn't spoken in the year since she showed up on their doorstep with an infant begging them to take her so that she wouldn't have to put her in foster care. She'd made that threat knowing her parents would never have that in hopes that they would accept Lacey and they had. To her dismay, her mother initially said no, but seeing how helpless she was, her father convinced her to let the baby stay.

Marissa had promised to come back for Lacey shortly, but she never did. She didn't know if she'd ever be able to go back to get her daughter. At this point, her mother would probably fight her to keep Lacey out of her hands. Her father had already let her know that her mother had gone to court to get custody of Lacey when Marissa failed to return to get her. That had been six months ago and she never contested. Lacey was in the right place because her own life was in shambles. She couldn't care for an infant while living her life on a pole every night.

"How can you ask that your mother forgive you when you won't forgive yourself? William asked.

"You know who I am, daddy. You know what I do. You may say you forgive me, but I can't see how you could or would. I'm nothing like the daughter you hoped you were raising. I'm not that same Marissa anymore," she said, softly.

"You will always be Marissa and I don't care what you're calling yourself these days. You are and always will be my daughter and I love you. You need to come home. If your mother won't forgive you, I have and so has God. He loves you and it doesn't matter to Him how far you've fallen. It's never too far down that He won't reach out with His loving arms and pull you back into His embrace. Home is not the only place you will find love and forgiveness. He's already forgiven you, but you have to forgive yourself, come part of the way and let God lead you the rest of the way," he asserted.

Marissa began to cry thinking about her plight. She heard the words, but wasn't sure she believed that God could love someone like her. There were days when she looked at herself in the mirror and found it hard to forgive herself. How could God or anyone else forgive and love the person she'd become – what she'd become?

"He loved the girl I was, but the woman I am right now is not loveable by God or anyone else. Ask mom," she said, referencing the harsh words her mother would speak to her at times when she called home and her mother answered the phone. With her, the call was always brief, followed by the clicking of her hanging up or she would pass the phone to her father, the only line to her family that was still in place. She and her mother never could have a civil conversation and with time, that had only gotten worse.

"I will always love you and so does your mother, even in her anger, so trust that. God has loved you from the moment you took your first breath and He still does today. Trust His love and His word that He can bring you out."

Marissa wiped her tears and knew that she needed to end the call. Standing in the hallway crying would soon draw someone's attention and could lead to more trouble if she were found in the school illegally.

"I hear you, daddy. I'll call again soon. Can you kiss Lacey for me and tell her I love her? I will try to get to

Philly to see her soon. I love you," she said, rushing him off the phone.

"I love you and never forget that. Always remember that God loves you, too."

Marissa nodded even though he couldn't see it. She wasn't sure she could get any words out.

"Bye, daddy."

She hung up before he could respond. She needed to have a good cry and standing in the middle of a high school where she shouldn't be wasn't the place to do that.

As she ran down the hall toward the exit to get back to her car, she cried softly, mumbling to herself.

"No, God doesn't love me. He couldn't. Why would He? I've shamed my family and turned my back on Him years ago. No, he wouldn't welcome me back and say yes to Delilah. Maybe to Marissa, but I'm not that young girl anymore. I'm now Delilah and no one loves her. Men desire her and others enjoy making money off of her, but no one genuinely loved her. She didn't even love herself anymore. She was lost and wouldn't be found because no one was looking. They weren't looking for Marissa because she no longer existed. Delilah, on the other hand was wanted and needed by many and she struggled with giving up how that made her feel.

Busting through the school doors, she ran as fast as she could as tears blurred her vision. The more she wiped them away, the harder they fell. She wished she could run and escape the life she'd chosen. She didn't know a way out. There was no one in the wings willing to rescue her.

3

Roman groaned as he rolled from one side of his king-sized bed to the other, resisting any attempt to get up in order to get Nina to school on time. Any minute, he was expecting his six-year old ball of early morning fire to come barging into his room asking if could she have waffles for breakfast, a meal she loved just about every single morning. As a police officer who worked the overnight shift in Philadelphia, he usually stayed awake after his shift until he returned from dropping her off at school and then he'd rush home to catch a few hours of sleep before it was time to pick her up late in the afternoon. If she didn't have any after school activities they needed to jet off to, they would come home, do homework and she'd spend an hour asking him all kinds of questions as they ate dinner. His sister, Sherri, who as a full-time college student in her junior year, lived with them and was home evenings and overnight with Nina when he left to go to work. She was a big help and so were his parents who lived a few miles away.

This morning was a different kind of morning

because he'd made a switch with another officer who needed two days off for family time and asked to work a double shift. In turn, he got a break from his own overnight shift policing the streets of Philadelphia, a city he loved and believed that there was no better place to live and raise Nina, who was growing by leaps and bounds every day. He loved his little butterfly and though he knew he shouldn't, he spoiled her without shame. He was just as dedicated to his job as he was to her, hoping to make the world a better place for her to live in as she grew and matured. The streets of Philly could be brutal and he did everything in his power to keep her and the citizens in the city of brotherly love as safe as possible.

Times when he thought too hard about it, he longed to do something else. The job was strenuous on his mind, body and spirit with everything he encountered. There were days when he wondered if he was meant to do something other than risk his life, possibly making his daughter an orphan if he made one slip up that could cost him his life. Criminals no longer feared the law or going to jail and wouldn't think twice about the value of his life, especially when they didn't value their own.

Thinking he may have at least one more snooze to get through, he reached for the clock and instead of hitting the button, his left hand strayed to the right and he knocked the photo that sat next to the clock onto the floor where it slammed loudly. His body went into protective mode, sitting straight up, now wide awake. He whipped the comforter off of himself and reached down to the floor to pick up the picture and prayed the glass had not cracked. Nervously, he turned on the lamp, illuminating the room that was still cast in darkness because of the early morning hour before daylight.

Taking a moment to pause and calm his fast beating heart while holding his breath, he turned the picture over, checking it until he was sure the picture frame remained intact by running his fingers across the uncracked glass that covered his favorite photo of him and Melanie from their wedding day ten years ago when they were twenty-one years old. She was the girl he'd loved since he was a little runny-nosed kid in elementary school back in Washington, D.C. where they both grew up. He smiled at the memories that flooded his mind of the good years they shared together.

Seeing her beautiful face, he thought back to that day many, many years ago when as a nine-year old, he'd spent months pulling Melanie's long ponytails, getting in trouble and being sent to the principal's office. When his father had to pick him up from school so that he could meet with the principal, he knew he was going to be in for another one of his long lectures about keeping his hands to himself. The next day, he thought Melanie would be angry at him for taunting her the day before, but instead, she walked by his table at lunch and gave him a cupcake. When she walked away smiling and waving, he knew they were meant to be, even at that age.

They went through elementary and middle school together and then one day before they were to start high school, his father told him that as a family, they were moving to Philadelphia because of a job transfer. The only thing that mattered to him was that he would be leaving Melanie and he couldn't imagine life without her. He didn't know what he would do if they no longer lived a block away from each other.

Family and friends thought that they would eventually grow out of being boyfriend and girlfriend, but they never did and the move devastated them. They promised to stay in contact and keeping that promise, when his family finally realized how serious he was about Melanie, his father allowed him to travel to Washington in order to be Melanie's date for both her junior and her senior prom and she in turn traveled with her family to Philadelphia for his junior and senior proms, too. It was funny to him how their relationship turned into a family affair.

After graduating high school, Melanie decided to go on to college while he decided to go into the army, again separating them. After one year in, at nineteen, he found himself proposing marriage to her one day while he was home visiting and then two years later, they were married and moved to a military base in Kansas. Melanie was able to enroll in college and for a few years, while he went from one country to another on tour, Melanie held down their home in Kansas.

One day right before he was thinking of re-enlisting, she had come home to tell him she had confirmed with her doctor that she was pregnant. They were over the hill with excitement knowing that they had always talked about having a big family. Melanie had been an only child and he and his sister, Sherri were his parents' only children.

Then one day, just before he was set to sign on for his next four-year stint in the military, during one of Melanie's routine checks, her doctor had found a lump in her breast after she complained about pain she assumed was attributed to her pregnancy. It wasn't and from that point on, their lives were a whirlwind. While consulting with doctors, they were told that the treatment for the cancer she would have to endure would mean that she would lose the baby. After days of them talking, he agreed that the decision would be hers and he would support whatever she wanted to do. Melanie wanted to have their baby and if for some reason, she didn't survive, he would always have a part of her that would live and thrive. He decided not to re-enlist so that he could have time with his family when he was needed the most.

To be closer to family, they made the move to Philadelphia to be closer to his parents who could help with Melanie and with the baby after she gave birth. Melanie's parents weren't too far away and made the drive to Philadelphia from Washington, D.C. often. Her mother sometimes came and stayed for weeks while her husband held down their home and worked, traveling back and forth almost weekly. Melanie's treatment for the cancer was put off until after Nina was born, which happened about six weeks before her actual due date. Melanie's body couldn't stand the weight of the baby and the tumors that continued to ravage her body and so Nina's birth was induced a few weeks early. They had tried one treatment after another, but the assessment was that the cancer had spread and Melanie lived a year after Nina arrived.

Roman leaned on his faith through the trials of Melanie's illness while at the same time, making sure his daughter got the love and attention she needed from him.

He had been raised in the church and even when he and Melanie moved to Kansas, they had found a church where they could worship together whenever he was home. At times when he was away, he tried to stay close to the ministry and appreciated times when his pastor or a member of the intercessory ministry would call, email or text a prayer or scriptures to him to keep his spirits lifted.

The church members were great to Melanie while he was away and once she was diagnosed with cancer and the pregnancy, every day someone from the church checked in on her or asked if they could help in any way. After their move to Philadelphia, their pastor in Kansas referred them to a church where he thought they would fit in and Brownstone Gospel Fellowship Church was the perfect place for them.

Today, as a deacon at the church and head of security, he enjoyed being in a leadership position and having a church that was like extended family. His pastor, Dr. Lorenda Battle, was one of the most inspirational pastors in Philadelphia and through her teaching and preaching, he was able to survive losing Melanie. His heart had experienced a pain he never thought possible when he lost her, but his church family was right there to make sure he stayed strong. The Bible got him through many bouts of self-pity he'd experienced, but he also knew he had a job to do. He loved the Lord and didn't make a move without God's guidance.

In ministry, Nina also flourished. She had grown from a baby into a beautiful six-year-old little darling who carried his heart with her wherever she went. He loved that they were a part of a church where she could be active in sports, dance and singing. She played on the church's little league softball and basketball teams, playing against other churches on Saturday mornings. During the week, she had dance and choir rehearsal along with meeting weekly with her girl scout troop. He'd made a promise to Melanie that their daughter would love the church, love the Lord and have fun enjoying life. That was a promise he made sure to fulfill. The only activity she was involved in that wasn't directly connected to the church was cheerleading. For that, he'd signed her up at a local recreation center where he also volunteered his time working as an assistant coach to the little league football team. He liked that they kept busy and though they missed Melanie, he enjoyed finding the time to allow Nina to explore activities that interested her.

Besides being a police officer, a coach and a deacon at his church, he spent a lot of his time giving back to his church and community. Along with another police officer who was a member of his church, together they were responsible for the church's security ministry team of over twenty men and women. A large team was necessary when it came to the large church ministry of over five thousand members. He was thankful for the opportunity to have his time occupied as he raised his daughter after Melanie no longer had the strength to hold or feed her. He knew the time she had with Nina before she died was precious to her and not wanting to miss out on even a second of Nina's life, she chose to live out her last months in the comfort of their home with him and Nina close by. He was thankful for the year Melanie was able to have loving and bonding with Nina until the end.

Following Melanie's death, their lives had changed. There was an emptiness not just in their home, but in their lives and though he appreciated the help his parents and his in-laws provided, nothing helped when it came to how much he missed the only woman he'd ever loved since before he knew what love was all about.

Roman turned back to the picture still in his hand, taken on the day they were married, one of the greatest days of his life. He kept the picture on the nightstand to remind him what that kind of love was like and wondered if God would send another woman with a beautiful spirit into his life. There were times when he questioned whether he wanted to bring someone into their lives or if he was meant to focus his attention on Nina, giving her double love for the parent she was missing. He'd tried dating a few times, but the schedule he kept prevented him from having a lot of time to invest in a serious relationship. There were many opportunities in the church and he never wanted to brag about the number of single women who approached him often, openly flirting, but none had him thinking of something beyond friendship. He didn't see himself as a casual dater, but he wanted a woman he could see himself falling in love with and marrying. He wouldn't be like other men he knew who used the church as a sensual playground. He missed his wife, but nothing would have him resorting to treating women with little to no respect.

Melanie made sure he knew that she expected him to find a woman that would love Nina as much as she does and he vowed that if God sent such a woman his way, he would be open to it wholeheartedly. He was nothing if he wasn't patient and he knew when God was ready to say yes to the perfect woman for him and Nina, he would know it.

He jumped the moment the alarm on his cellphone chimed letting him know it was time to get Nina up and off to school. He slipped into a sweat suit on the bench at the foot of the bed and rushed to make her breakfast, get her to school and then get himself back home for an afternoon of sleeping. He had a few days off to catch up on some rest. Thoughts of Melanie surfaced when he thought about the daily struggle of understanding God's decision to take her away. Why couldn't God say yes to him when that was what he wanted and needed the most? He had needed Melanie to get better, but that wasn't so. God had said, no.

4

Marissa sat in her sleek, four-door black BMW 650 in the parking lot beside the nightclub where she danced five nights a week in Trenton, New Jersey. She struggled with the thought of getting out of the car or putting it in drive and speeding away, never to look back again. She had thought about doing that many, many times, but then reality brought her back to her dilemma of having no place to go and, as she would tonight, end up going inside to once again become Delilah, her persona for the past eight years. Delilah was the woman she became at the age of eighteen when she thought her life as Marissa wasn't enough for her.

She looked up at the bright neon blue nightclub signage with an image of a scantily clad dressed woman holding a martini glass to her lips. The provocative looking woman is what drew the men to the club night after night and once inside, they encountered real women who dressed like that and were live and in living color – real flesh and blood women who were willing to do all sorts of things for the right price. She was no exception and the thought of hands of strangers touching her and slipping her bills for how she moved disgusted her.

Like most nights, her stomach turned in knots as she pulled up to the red brick building that had seen better days with many of the bricks damaged or missing. Out front, an old, worn and badly stained red carpet led the way to the steel black windowless door where Benny, one of the club bouncers stood as a towering figure projecting the aura that he was not to be played with. Knowing she had another hour before she was scheduled to grace the stage, she slumped back in her seat and did a quick assessment of how her life had come to the place where it was now.

She sulked as she wondered how she had gone from Marissa Ballard, the only daughter of two God-fearing parents who she now knew really loved her, but years ago, she didn't think so because she seemed to always disappoint them, to Delilah, a woman who took her clothes off and danced around for a bunch of nasty, freaky, dirty and often foul-smelling men several days a week. She could blame it on the money, which made it hard to give up, but it wasn't all about that because a portion of that went to the man who had introduced her to dancing and at one time, she thought actually loved her. She could blame it on the attention and the desirous looks she got from men who took delight in seeing more and more of her skin. She could also place blame on the fact that she had nothing else going for herself and this was all she knew. In actuality, there was no excuse for turning her back on the life she should have fought hard to maintain back in Philadelphia where she was born and had lived until she left one day after going through her final fight with her mother.

Since she was a little girl, she and her mother never got along. It didn't help that she'd had a child at twenty, dropped her off with them to raise and went back to her life in New Jersey. That move didn't help mend the brokenness between them, but for every year she stayed away, the wider the gap grew between them. She tried to get back to Philadelphia to see her daughter, but that always led to a big blow up with her mother and to avoid that, she stayed away. She went often enough that her six-year-old daughter, Lacey, knew who she was, but not enough to know that her absence was noticeable. She knew she couldn't go home and she hated the life she was living in Trenton, but sitting alone in her car, she realized she didn't have anyone. She was all alone and any way she looked at herself, everyone may find her beautiful, but she hated who she saw in her reflection. She wanted to be sick and tired enough to walk away from this life, but as of yet, she hadn't figured a way out. For eight years, this was her life day in and day out and for the first time earlier in the morning, she woke up wanting something else. The problem was, she didn't know what. Now would be the perfect time for someone to come along and shout at her to get it together and get out of Trenton.

Reaching down for her cell phone, she scrolled through the many names and numbers and realized there wasn't one name she could reach out to who would talk her down off the cliff. Her cliff was that dance floor and walking from her dressing room to center stage was like walking the green mile – her road to the death of her self-esteem, her pride and her faith in who she knew she could be if she took a leap of faith. Somewhere with the passage of each day, her self-esteem looked further and further away and she'd lost any that she had night after night, leaving it on the dance floor. She found herself at the edge of a cliff every evening when it was time for her to go out on the dance floor. That wasn't her only cliff.

Another cliff was the walk across the hardwood floors of the apartment she lived in with a man who wanted her for her body and the money it brought him. Of course, she didn't want to leave out that her body wasn't the only one he'd been keeping his eyes on and hands on. More now than ever before, Wayne took no shame in strutting one young woman after another across their apartment, only to disappear into one of the two bedrooms with them. She would try to muffle the sounds that escaped the room that made her skin crawl and times when that wasn't enough, she would run out and drive around until she couldn't keep her eyes open any longer. She'd learned early to never question his actions, especially when it came to his amorous activities with other women. She tried not to question who she saw when she looked in the mirror every day. She wondered what kind of woman would put up with the kind of treatment he dished out regularly. This is a man she ran away with eight years ago after promises of the good, high life, but one who in reality, kept her stagnate and bowing to his every whim, no matter how degrading it was for her. At one time, she thought she was in love, but she quickly learned love had nothing to do with what he wanted from her. His focus was on the amount of money her nightly activities brought in to him. That wasn't love – it was possession. She often heard people say it, but she never wanted to believe it – she was his property to do with how he chose. Where had things gone so wrong?

Looking up at the club again, she noticed a crowd had formed at the entrance and she knew that one of the reasons was her. She was the club's biggest draw on the nights that she danced and she had to admit, the money was great. At this point, what choice did she have but to get out of her car and go do what she was good at. This was her world, her life now and to do anything but this would be foreign and out of place for her. She never dreamed the young girl who loved to dance would end up using that talent on a stripper pole.

Every day, she was becoming more like Delilah and

less like Marissa, the woman who once had big dreams and high hopes for herself as a professional dancer. From elementary to high school, she received accolades for her natural dance ability and she was filled with dreams of stardom. How had she let herself fall this far? What happened to that young girl who went to church every Sunday, was a member of the youth dance team, marched around as an usher and enjoyed singing on the choir? Where was that student whose grades were so high that she received a four-year academic college scholarship and one for dance, something she only partially took advantage of before she hightailed it out of Philadelphia after meeting Wayne and letting him convince her that they were going to live like a king and queen in New Jersey?

Now, here she was, taking her clothes off for strange men. She was meant for more than this. Marissa knew if she was thinking about how bad her life was, she had to also be thinking about what the good life would have been like if she'd done the right thing instead of always trying to battle with her parents over the path they wanted her to take. She was depressed thinking how the person she had become had embarrassed her family to the point that when she did find time to go home to visit Lacey, she never stayed more than a day or two, knowing that her mother sneered at her every chance she got, treating her like a servant asking her to use the entrance to their house in the back. She didn't blame her. No one would want to claim a daughter who stripped for a living, especially not the Christ-like, bible toting parents she had. This was her life and with as much as she hated it, she grabbed her things from the passenger seat of the car and stepped out in her five-inch heels. She still had a job to do. There was money to make.

Instead of walking through the front door where she would be accosted by one man after the other before she even made it to her dressing room, she walked around the side of the building to the entrance only club employees used. Pulling the hood of her sweatshirt over her head, she held her bags close and walked quickly, keeping her identity hidden from those who looked her way. She knocked on the door and within seconds it was opened by another one of the club's bouncers.

"Hey Delilah," he said and she cringed. Though it was her stage name, she hated hearing it come out of anyone's mouth. The name reminded her of who she was in everyone's eyes.

She mumbled a hello and keeping her head down, she walked the short distance to the dressing room where she quickly changed into the silver and white, rhinestone clad bikini outfit she was planning to wear for her first set of the night.

"Delilah, you're up next on the main stage, so get moving."

She jumped hearing her name being called and

knowing who was calling it, she felt sick. She hated Klaus, the old white man who owned the club and who made her feel even dirtier with the way he said her name, in a slurred, demeaning way. So many called her by that name that she herself often forgot it wasn't her given name.

What is it about that name? Every time anyone said it, she was reminded of the trashy persona associated with it. She shouldn't complain because it wasn't like she wanted her birth name associated with the life she's now living or the performance she was about to give. When she turned to the dressing room door, Klaus was standing there waiting for her to acknowledge him. She hated that he would open the door without even knocking and a few times, he had actually walked in catching her or one of the other dancers completely naked. Even now, she could have been in between outfits and she would have been vulnerable to his menacing, alcohol-induced red eyes. Her hatred of him was real.

"Yeah, yeah. I'll be ready. You can leave now," she said without emotion, hoping to dismiss him.

Turning back to the mirror hoping he'd do a disappearing act, she picked up the purple eyeshadow to complete the face that was Delilah, exotic dancer extraordinaire. Instead of Klaus leaving, her back stiffened when his wrinkled, old face appeared in the mirror above hers. The moment his fat, rough, steely hands touched her bare shoulders, she practically leaped out of the chair to get away from him, stumbling nervously in her high, clear, glass stilettos.

"Whoa, what's with all the hostility?" he asked. "This is a friendly reminder that you're up next," he added.

She tried to ignore the sinister grin he used and thought women found attractive. What they often found attractive was his money, something that didn't appeal to her. Whenever she danced, he would toss a few hundred-dollar bills at her, but she felt like trash the minute she bent down to pick up the wet, wadded up bills from the floor.

"I answered you, so why are you still here?" she declared loudly looking around noticing the other girls who were in the room when she arrived were already out on the floor. For her act, Klaus liked for the other girls to be on the floor entertaining the men while she performed on stage. She was his hottest act and the biggest draw for men every night she was on stage.

"I heard that. I was just wondering what you were doing after the show tonight? You've been dancing here for a few years and we've never had the chance to enjoy a nice dinner together. Maybe a private show just for old Klaus? You know, I can double and even triple whatever you get in tips tonight from the crowd. What do you say?" he said walking toward where she moved beyond the dressing table.

Marissa was frightened. Klaus made passes at all

the girls and she knew most took him up on his offer of dinner and extra, but not her; never her. As he came closer, she panicked noticing there was no place to go. Behind her was a brick wall and no exit. He was so large, there was no way of getting around him without their bodies actually touching. Scantily clad, she didn't like the position he was placing her in where she couldn't move out of his reach. He was blocking the door and even if she screamed for help, no one would hear her over the loud music.

"I'm busy after the show," she stuttered out while reaching down to close the robe over her skimpy outfit. She felt even more exposed when his eyes traveled back and forth, up and down her body.

"You sure are pretty. I'm wondering why we've never spent any time together and you know I'd like a date."

The creepy look in his eyes was one she'd seen before and she'd been warned by the other girls to stay away from him. She was his big money maker, so he'd never been inappropriate with her, but she had a feeling he didn't care much about being appropriate anymore. The look in his eyes said something else. Marissa shook nervously the closer he moved to her, invading her space to the point where she could feel his hot, garbage smelling breath on her face.

"I have to get ready for my show, Klaus," she said.

"I got that. Let's talk after your set and see if you can somehow free up your night for Klaus. After all, it's because of me that you have that flashy car and all that bling you girls like to show off. Surely, I can get a little of your time?" he snickered.

Klaus moved, boxing her in.

Marissa found her back up against the coldness of the wall and terror overcame her when she knew she wasn't going to be able to get away.

"She said she was busy!" a boisterous voice said from the doorway like a boom from a pair of drums.

She and Klaus looked over at the door together as Wayne's large six-foot-five, four-hundred-pound body filled the entire frame. He was a massive figure that no one ever wanted to go up against. She knew that there were still a few bodies that were connected to him that had never been found of men and women who had disrespected him or come for him. Wayne terrorized everyone and even Klaus knew when to back down. Though he ran the club, Wayne ran the people in the club and that included Klaus who stepped away from her fast, practically stumbling over his own feet tiny feet that were not proportionate with his size. His pasty white face was now a bright red color. He may have been the man in charge, but Wayne was the beast in charge and no one ever questioned him. When he spoke, everyone listened and moved with a swiftness.

"Sorry, Wayne. I was reminding Delilah that she was up next on the main stage," Klaus said sheepish-like.

Wayne moved further into the room rubbing his hands together as if he were about to pounce. She knew the signs of Wayne reaching his limit and the moment he reached up and grasped, then rubbed his full-bearded chin while sucking on his gold grill-covered teeth, she knew it was time to make a quit exit, but now both men blocked the door.

"Is that right? You had to come all the way into the room to do that? You know Delilah is off limits to you at all times, even when she's not on the clock here. I don't care what you say or do with the other chicks around here, but lay a hand on Delilah and you will be figuring out how to eat with your feet. Don't ever let me here you make any reference to her car, bling or anything else she has. Just like all of those things, she belongs to me, too and don't you ever forget it. I bought everything she has and like I said, she belongs to me! Are we clear on that?" Wayne grimaced, looking down at Klaus as he towered over him.

The sweat on Klaus' head showed his fear and hers, too. What was Wayne going to do and would she suffer by being in the line of fire? Her heart raced and where the room seemed cooler a minute ago, it was now as hot as a sauna.

"Yeah, we are," Klaus stuttered out while trying to make his way around Wayne, who moved so that no one was leaving until he was ready for them to leave.

"No, I want to hear that we are crystal clear – clear as a bright shiny day – clear as those glasses on your face before you started fogging them up with your nasty hot breath. I'm talking that kind of clear," Wayne said, meaning business.

Klaus' fear was evident and Wayne laughed at how he was able to turn the rich club owner into a wimpy bumbling idiot.

"Yeah, Wayne. We're clear on everything," Klaus said with terror in his voice.

"Cool. You can leave now and continue to stay away from Delilah. When I say she's mine, I mean it and never get it twisted again. She wasn't created for your grubby, fat little fingers. Now, be gone," he said dismissing Klaus with a swift wave of his hand which was three sizes larger than the average man's.

As Klaus made a quick dash exit for the door, she held her breath as Wayne turned his attention to her with a big, sinister smile, one that others may think showed genuine happiness, but she knew better. He was fuming inside at what he walked in on, her half naked with Klaus a little too close for comfort.

"I didn't do anything," she stumbled out before he accused her of anything. "I was getting ready for my show and he walked in uninvited without even knocking."

Explaining early usually kept her on Wayne's good side and without an extra bruise that she would need makeup to cover up.

"Don't sweat your pretty little head over that. I heard everything and you're good. He knows you're mine and I doubt he'll be any trouble. I knew he'd make a move one day and I decided to wait until that day to put a halt to any illusions he had about anything private with you. We're clear that you belong to me, right? You and everything about you belongs to me, right?" he asked, moving so close to her that she could no longer see beyond him. Her heart began to beat faster the minute he reached out and gripped her chin in his hand, lightly at first before tightening his grip causing a severe, sharp pain to radiate through her, shooting directly to her jaw which he now gripped tighter and tighter causing her to rise up on her toes, no easy feat in high heels.

"Yes," she uttered low, but loud enough for him to hear.

"Good. Now get that pretty behind of yours in gear. There's a big crowd out there tonight and they're all waiting on Delilah and I'm waiting on all the money you're going to make for us tonight," he snarled while releasing her face.

Without anything further, Wayne turned and left the dressing room, leaving her alone. She expected more and was glad it didn't happen. He appeared to be in a good mood which worked to her advantage. She was glad he hadn't made her pay for what Klaus tried to do. She would never take Klaus up on his offer and she didn't care how much money he threw at her. It was enough for her to stomach the men Wayne made her accommodate.

Remembering the door was unlocked, she walked over, closed it and then applied the lock to keep anyone else from entering. If any of the other girls needed to get in, they would have to wait.

Going back to her seat, she again picked up the make-up brush to finish applying her stage face when Wayne's words rang like a siren in her head. 'She belongs to me. You belong to me. She's mine.' All those were references to her.

"His?" she said to herself. "I'm not yours either. You may have created Delilah, but you didn't create who I am. Who am I?" she asked herself looking in the mirror. The image staring back at her was almost unrecognizable. Who was this young woman with the golden blond wig on her head and the fake green contacts in her eyes? Who was this young woman with the long, fake eyelashes on? This may be who she is now, but it's not who she wanted to be and one thing she wasn't was property or chattel. Had she really allowed Wayne to believe he owned her? He had bought her the new BMW she drove and the platinum, diamond and gold jewelry she wore. He'd provided all the fine clothes and the expensive apartment she lived in with him, but did that mean he owned her?

The music blared and the light in her dressing room beamed bright to let her know she had ten more minutes and then it was stage time. Ignoring it, she put the make-up down without applying anymore and really looked at herself. Was Marissa Ballard still in there anywhere? Was she even her own person anymore? She went from being controlled by her parents to being controlled by this man. Why couldn't she figure out how to assert control her own life?

She thought over how her show typically went and for the first time, she felt sickened at being entertainment for a bunch of nasty young and old men who touched, groped and spoke vile things to her, all for the thrill of watching her humiliate herself for the money they threw her way. They were no different than Wayne, a man she met who she thought loved her. A man who forced her to give up everything about herself, including her self-respect because he was able to convince her that as long as she had him, she didn't need self-respect, she only needed him. When did her need for someone else get so strong that she lost herself?

A tear trickled from her eye down her cheek as the weight of where her life was dropped down on her like a building that had just been imploded. This is not living, but it's all she had. Everyone who ever meant anything to her hated who she became and therefore wanted nothing to do with her.

She slammed her fist down hard on the glass dressing room table in disgust and impatience. Two men were in her dressing room tonight, both thinking she owed them enough to make them think they owned some piece of her. This wasn't her! This was Delilah, this wasn't Marissa.

Again, and again, she slammed her fist down on the glass table top.

"I can't take this anymore!" she shouted out loud as her body heaved uncontrollably in a motion that mimicked hyperventilating. Is this all there was for her? It couldn't be she thought. This couldn't be all there was for her.

She looked into the mirror and for the first time in a long time, she saw through Delilah and caught a glimpse of Marissa. She was still in there. Her lip trembled as she tried to hold back the tears. Her mouth opened to form words, but none came out. The action only caused more tears to fall from her eyes as her heart sank and sulked.

"I need a sign. This can't be it for me. I don't know how much more I can take," she cried to the image in the mirror.

Marissa looked over at the razor blade she used to trim her eyebrows and thought of another use for it that she'd struggled with over the past few years.

As tears began to fall harder and her body began to shake uncontrollably, the air in the room grew thick. She tried to hold the tears back by holding her breath until she realized that meant not breathing. Maybe that's what needs to happen. Maybe I need to stop breathing, she thought. She held her breath and didn't let it go until her eyes grew so big from no air, she knew she had to release it. She reached for the razor and thought of how quickly she could make all of her pain end.

What happened next wasn't just a release of the breath she was holding, but it was a release of everything she'd been keeping in that made her hate who she was. She suddenly dropped the razor and let it clink to the floor. This wasn't her. An image of Lacey gleamed bright in her mind. A razor wasn't her way out.

Shocking herself, she screamed and let out a holler from her belly that reminded her of when she was a little girl in church when her mother would say a holler like that was pushing out demons and letting them know they had no place in a body that belonged to God. Her mother once told her all she had to do was call out to God for help and he would get her out of any situation she'd gotten herself into as long as she was open to trusting Him. He could rescue her from herself.

She screamed and pushed and screamed and pushed and then looked at herself in the mirror, seeing her tear-stained face where her makeup had run black from her eyes in terrifying streaks. She felt alone, she looked alone. Her body shook in terror as the image in the mirror that had shown her a little of Marissa was now filled completely with Delilah and her world crashed. She gripped the edge of the glass table and held on so tight, she felt the pain in her hands.

"I...I...I..need help! Help me!" she hollered. "Help

me!" she screamed. "HELP ME!" she bellowed. "Help me!" she shouted. "Help me!" she bawled. *HELP ME!*

"It's Marissa, it's not Delilah. My name is Marissa Ballard," she screamed at the mirror, where instead of seeing herself, she saw the faces of all the men she let touch her who had no right to. She saw Wayne's face, the man with whom she shared a child and wasn't allowed to raise because he only wanted Delilah the dancer, not Marissa the woman. His face was of a man she thought loved her, but love wouldn't have her doing some of the most disgusting things a woman could do at a man's request.

"Are you okay in there?"

Marissa jumped at the sound of Crystal's voice on the other side of the dressing room door. One of the other dancers needed to get in the room.

"Delilah?" Crystal called out.

"Stop calling me that," she said under her breath. "My name is Marissa."

She said it so low, no one would have heard her. She looked around to see if there was a sign somewhere of what she needed to do to get out of the life that was tearing her down. She screamed, she pushed, she asked for help, yet she didn't see any help. She wondered where was this God her mother had always told her about? He wasn't showing up to help her when she needed him the most. She didn't feel any different. She didn't see anything happening. There was no lightning flashing or no thunder rolling. She should have known that there wasn't a God who would love the person she was today. She was still the same Marissa, who tonight, was called Delilah. Even as Crystal continued to call out to her from the other side of the door, she struggled with what to do next.

Feeling her body calm, she knew the answer. There wasn't going to be any help for her. Like all church people do, her mother had lied to her about a God she claims only needed to hear a plea for help and help would be on the way. She looked around the room and all she saw was what she'd always seen – the place where her dreams continued to die night after night. Feeling stupid for thinking there was some majestic help out there somewhere that would rescue her from her pitiful life, she shrugged off the thought and decided to be content with the fact that this was her life and it always would be. There was no one and especially no God who would help her. She had to keep on using what she had to get what she wanted.

"Well, there goes all that churchy wisdom my mother tried to sway me with. No help for me I guess," she said, feeling the weight of all of her problems on her shoulders. She looked down at the floor. "I'm sure I'll see you again, razor," she scoffed.

"Delilah!" Crystal again screamed her name.

Wiping her face and fixing her makeup as best she could, she walked over and opened the door.

"Hey, Crystal," she said with a straight face, pulling it together.

"Girl, what were you doing in here? I thought I heard you scream."

"Nothing, just getting ready for my show," she lied.

"Let's go then. You know I make my best tips when you're on stage. We need you, girl," Crystal said and proceeded to help her finish getting ready by fixing the make-up that had been smeared on her face with tears.

When Crystal didn't ask any questions about the tears, she knew that she wasn't the only one who had been where she is. The problem was, the same way she ignored her down-trodden life, Crystal was doing the same.

"I'm ready to make this money now," Delilah said checking herself in the mirror.

For a split second, she remembered seeing Marissa again and then Crystal showed up and reminded her that she's Delilah, Tuesday through Saturday night.

"I guess this is who I'm supposed to be," she said.

"What?" Crystal asked, puzzled.

Marissa shrugged her shoulders, stiffened her back and got into character.

"Nothing. I was talking to myself about something I thought would happen, but didn't. Let's go get this money!" she said, standing tall and holding her head up. "I guess if I'm going to have to continue helping myself, I'd better get back to my reality and not some fantasy of leaving this life behind," she said to herself.

She saw the perplexed look on Crystal's face and

smiled to distract her. She turned and left the dressing room with Crystal in tow.

As she was about to take the stage after hearing herself as Delilah being announced, Marissa had no clue that in the quiet of the room she'd walked out of after pleading for help, the lights had suddenly blown out. They didn't just burn out or blow out with a crackle, but they exploded, sending the room into total darkness as shards of glass littered the floor. As Delilah began her show, turning, grinding and twisting to the sounds of a slow R&B song, things were already happening in her favor and she was unaware. There was no way for her to know that her future was about to be altered and the plan for her life was going to be made crystal clear. Delilah swayed and dipped not knowing that the lights on 'Delilah' had just gone dark, but she wasn't in the room to witness the beginning of her answered prayer. She didn't wait for God to move on her behalf, though He would do so anyway. She'd had a little faith and then replaced it with doubt. That little bit of faith was all it took for the God of grace and mercy to answer her prayer. Unbeknownst to her, it wasn't the only time God would show up. He'd heard her and He was still in the blessing business. God was on a mission to rescue her because after all that she'd been through, she had finally asked for His help and He was listening.

5

Another shift was over and Roman wasn't in a rush to get home in order to get Nina off to school. He turned when he heard one of his friends talking to him as he stuffed his uniform into his bag before leaving the precinct and heading to the gym for a few hours to lift weights. He had the morning and afternoon free since Nina was with his parents for a few days. His mother was going to take Nina shopping for a dress for a birthday party that was coming up in a few days. Having extra time, he wanted to use it at the gym, a place he hadn't been able to make it to lately.

"I can't believe the call I got last night," Moe said in a loud and boisterous voice.

"What is it now, Moe?" he asked.

He and Moe had been friends since the first day they had joined the force together. After moving from Kansas, he wasn't sure of the career path he would go in after leaving the military to care for his wife, but when he arrived back in Philadelphia, he had seen a sign recruiting for the police department and he knew with his military background, he would be good on the force and he needed a job. He now considered being an officer as a chosen career for him, but back then, it was a means for him to take care of his growing family. Silently, he thought about the fact that he had been questioning if his job was really a career for him anymore.

"Janice called and said your date ended early the other night. What's up with that? I hooked you up with a beautiful woman and you don't call her back after the first date. What's up with that?" he asked.

Roman didn't know the conversation they were having was going to be about the date he'd had with a friend of Moe's, but now that it was, he wasn't going to be able to avoid it.

"I didn't get a vibe that she was the one," Roman explained and tried to ignore Moe's stare.

Moe laughed out loud.

"Bruh, the one? You're out here looking for the one? I hooked you up with Janice to be Ms. Right Now, not Ms. One. She was in the Wiz, the black version of The Wizard of Oz," he chuckled. "I didn't find "the one" for your date. You need to have some kind of life outside of work and caring for Nina. Do you even remember what it's like to date?" Moe asked.

"Funny. I know you're being a wise guy, but I'm being serious. You know I'm not looking to casually date and everything about Janice said casual. Throughout the whole date, she did everything to get me to go back to her place and spend the night which is code for booty call. I'm not looking for a woman being comfortable being a booty call. I'm looking for that special spark, that connection and I didn't get that. She was beautiful and all that, but a woman should be more than that and know that she's more than that. Janice doesn't know that."

"Her body was everything wasn't it?" Moe asked.

Roman shook his head and smiled. He couldn't be angry at Moe for being who he was and knew that as friends, they could talk about everything. Unlike him, Moe was a man all about the ladies and to him, the more the better. His own thoughts were far from that which is why he had a few other friends who also tried to set him up on dates. He knows it's been five years since Melanie died and just two years ago, he finally removed his wedding band and put it away in the safe he kept at home. He'd love to be in love again, but he didn't want to go the casual route to get there. The atmosphere for dating these days was one that gave him pause because too many women didn't have high enough expectations and men had no problem obliging them. He meant it when he said he was looking for more and wanted a woman who wanted more from him than amorous activities in bed. He was still a man and had urges, but his heart wanted more than the desires of his body.

"She was gorgeous, but I need more than that and when I asked her what church she went to, she told me she doesn't believe in God. That date was over as soon as those words came out of her mouth. I may not be an angel, but I am a child of God and I can't date a woman who doesn't believe. That kind of relationship isn't going anywhere."

"Relationship? Man, who said anything about a relationship? All I was doing was trying to help my brother out with some action."

Roman laughed.

"I don't need you finding me action and women should be looked at as more than that. I think we both know if I was looking for action, I wouldn't have a problem getting it," Roman said.

"Right because how many times have you been asked to join that calendar of Philly's finest? I'm still waiting to be asked once and they've done everything, but bribed you to be featured, even offering you the cover. Two years in a row and you've been the number one pick, yet you won't do it. Sales would be through the roof if you said yes. Everybody wants Roman, but Roman is out here waiting on "the one"."

Moe laughed out loud and slammed the locker shut and stood to leave.

"Come on, Moe, you didn't meet me yesterday. You know the kind of guy I am. I'm looking for more than a pretty face and someone who's willing to take me back to her place to spend the night on the first date. I appreciate the gesture, but no more hookups. When I'm ready to date, I still know how to do it. I still got it. As far as that calendar is concerned, I'm thinking about it for this next go 'round only because they have agreed to donate the profits this year to several shelters and transitional houses around town and you know I'm all about that. My family runs one and could use the help of all this money they claim the calendar could raise. I'm waiting for the cause to be right and I also want to be sure they don't have an expectation of me being shirtless. I will never agree to that."

"Man, shirt or no shirt, they know the women will eat that calendar up with you on the cover. I'm just glad you let me be in your space to take all these thirsty women off your hands that you throw back!" Moe exclaimed.

Roman shook his head. He loved their banter, but also knew Moe meant every word.

"There really is no hope for you, is there?" Roman asked, laughing out loud.

"I can't help myself. I'm the opposite of you. Keep praying for a brother! For now, if you change your mind, Janice wants to see you again or if you prefer another flavor, I got you."

"I think I'm good, but you go ahead and do you."

"Are you sure? I'm saying, you spend all of your time with Nina, at church or at the community center helping out with those kids. You need some real adult fun and I've known Janice for a long time. She's good people, but yeah, she can be a little fast."

Roman looked at Moe sideways.

"A little fast? Dude, as soon as we sat down to eat,

she wanted to know if we could take the food out, stop and get some ice cream and whipped cream at the store and go back to her house for the rest of the night and see what we could get into. Those were her exact words accompanied with a look that brought the idea home. As tempting as that is since I am a man, that's not who I am. When I date, I want her to be wife material. I'm not looking to marry her off the back, but I want the woman I have a second date with to be someone I found on the first date to have the qualities I love in a woman. Janice was nice, but she's far from wife material. She's out for the enjoyment and trust me, I'm not judging."

"Yeah, I know. I was trying to help you have some fun. I can see the look on your face on days when you're really missing Melanie. No one can put a timeframe on when you should move on and I'm not trying to force that. I want to see you happy again and lately, you've been down in the dumps. Is everything alright with you?" Moe asked.

"Everything is good, but there are days when I'm wondering what I'm doing. I mean, I love my life and raising Nina is my everything, but I can't help but feel like something is missing, not in my life, but with what I'm doing with my life. These streets are getting crazy and people are more fearless than ever. It's a lottery every day we step in those streets in our uniforms and I've wondered about the real difference we should be making, but aren't. The people don't trust us anymore and I'm not just talking about here in Philly, but everywhere across the country. This world has taken God out of so much that there isn't even a semblance of human decency anymore."

"I hear you. I hear a lot of our brothers and sisters in blue saying the same thing and wondering if the sacrifice is worth it. No one loves helping people more than you do. We all love what we do, but you're different. You actually want to be able to touch, feel and see an actual change in what we do and it's not happening. You're that person who wants to rescue everyone. You can't take on the problems of the world. Do what you can and go home to your daughter after every shift. The goal every day is to go home at the end of the day. Don't lose sight of that in trying to fix the world. Don't let it weigh you down. You are making a difference even if you can't see it. If no one else around here is, you definitely are. This is why I'm trying to get the right woman in your space to get that fogginess out of your head. You're thinking too hard instead of getting back into the swing of things as a single guy. One more hookup. What do you say?" Moe asked.

"I have plenty of fun and trust me, when I come across the kind of woman I'm looking for, you'll be the first to know. Stop trying to hook me up. Now, are you heading to the gym with me or do I have to continue to sit through more of your judgement?" he quipped.

"Yeah, yeah – I'm going to the gym. Let me fill out

this report on this arrest I made before the end of the shift and I'll meet you there."

Roman nodded as he grabbed his duffle bag and headed out to his car. Talking about women with Moe had him thinking about how he'd been so focused on everyday life, he didn't realize he had practically given up on dating. He had found other things to fill his time. His sister told him he needed to get back out there and when he least expected it, a woman he never thought would be for him is going to blow his mind. He doubted her, but he understood where she was coming from.

He and God had been having chats lately about how empty his life felt on days when he didn't know what direction his life was supposed to go in. He knew his job was to take care of his daughter, but what about him? What else was there for his life? Was he ready for a new woman to enter his life? To enter Nina's life? He'd made a promise and though his heart was still hurting, there had to be an out for him. He had to break free from the doldrum that had become his life and find that thing that was more for him. Was it time for him to open his heart to another woman? Would he find that perfect woman who brought about a change that was needed or should he take Moe's advice and just get back out there and enjoy being single?

Roman knew he had to be the only man in the world turning down woman after woman for one fling after another. He'd been tempted like any other red, hot-blooded man on the planet, but when he thought about the drama it could lead to, he wasn't for that. He loved the love he had with Melanie and knew it was still out there for him in another woman. Was he looking for one to rescue him from the loneliness he felt in his heart? He wasn't sure, but he knew five years had been enough time of fighting rejoining everyday life.

6

Marissa drove down the familiar Philadelphia street much slower than the posted speed limit. Her nerves were ragged as she anticipated an encounter that in the past, had not gone well. This street held more memories for her than any other, yet she felt like a stranger as she passed by houses where friends she grew up with lived. These were houses where she played as a little girl and celebrated birthday parties. Once she turned on to the street of her childhood home, she should have felt a sense of peace, but her feelings were far from that. She felt antsy, jumpy and a little spooked at the possibility of being spotted by someone.

Her parents had lived in their home for over thirty years and everyone knew everyone on the block. She had no doubt they knew her story even if her mother hadn't told it, which she was sure she had not. The last thing her mother would ever want is for her neighbors to know that her daughter claimed being a stripper as a career. Her parents were ashamed of her or at least her mother was. Her father never said much about what she did with her life unless she brought up the subject first and his emotions were often unreadable. She stayed away so that she wouldn't have to see disappointment staring back at her when she saw them. Today was a different kind of day. She didn't have any place to go, no one she could call on and the only person she truly missed was on the other side of the door at her parents' house. If she wanted to see her, she would have to face her mother. Her feelings of being, compunctious and riddled with guilt and regret wouldn't keep her from standing her ground with her mother. Today was that day. She wanted to see Lacey.

Finding a parking spot a few houses down, Marissa exited her car and nervously straighten her clothes. Her attire could be better, but she'd come right from Newark to Philadelphia and didn't bother to change. Even if she had slept in her car all night, she didn't want to look like she had, but her clothes didn't matter to her right now.

On shaky legs, she walked the short distance to her parents' house where the grass was neatly trimmed and the rose bushes her mother loved so much in pink, red and white were blooming beautifully. She looked up at the eight steps to the door and remembered the fun she had as a child playing on them as well as the strong-will she had the day she proclaimed she was leaving and would never return, running down those steps with her few possessions in her arms. What stood out most about that day was the moment she turned around and hoped beyond hope that either her mother or father would call her back and explain how they could work things out, but that didn't happen. Not only did they not call out after her, but when she turned around after leaving the front door wide open when she ran out, someone had closed the door and no one stood there. Her last thought as she looked at the house that day was that they were probably happier that she was leaving than she was.

Climbing the stairs, Marissa took several deep breaths before ringing the doorbell. She waited and no one appeared. She didn't see either of their cars when she pulled up which didn't mean they weren't home. It could mean that they had parked their cars in the two-car garage in the back of the house. When no one answered after a minute, she was about to ring the bell again when the door slowly opened and on the other side of the storm door stood her mother, emotionless, with a face void of any expression at all at seeing her only child after months of no contact.

"Marissa, you can't be here," she said, something Marissa had expected.

Her heart sunk knowing that even though she should have expected the cold, icy greeting, she had prayed for something different this time.

"I'm not trying to cause any trouble, momma. I want to see Lacey, please," she said in a monotone voice as she kept her eyes on her mother's eyes, not breaking the stare. Like her mother, she could be stubborn and give as good as she received. If they were going to act like strangers, she could do that. She quickly softened her demeanor knowing she was at the mercy of her mother. She hoped that today would be the day that she would take pity on her and allow her to see her own child.

"You know you can't pop up anytime you want and demand to see her and besides, she's not here. Your father took her to ballet rehearsal at the church. Remember that place where you were raised to live a life nothing like the one you are living?" Martika Ballard scoffed.

Marissa cringed at the words her mother had pretty much spit out at her. She had expected it and took the lick. She held her composure and tried to stick to the reason why she was standing at their door. She wanted to see her daughter.

"Momma, not now," she said, hoping to change the direction of the conversation. "This isn't about that. This is about Lacey and I want to see her, I need to see her," she practically begged. "I've been going through something and I just need to see her, please," she added.

When her mother folded her arms across her chest, she had a feeling she wasn't going to be able to get through to her, at least not this day.

"Going through something? You're always going

through something and when you show up, we end up going through your drama with you. What are you doing up this early on a Saturday morning? You usually have a late Friday night, don't you?"

Marissa shivered at the abhorrent way she looked and spoke to her.

"I didn't come here to be judged as you tend to do every time you see me and yes, I remember church, but my question is, do you? Somewhere, I thought judging people was a sin. I didn't come here to get in a battle of wits with you and out of respect because you are my mother, I'll apologize for what I just said. Going at each other won't get us anywhere," she admitted.

"You have a lot that needs judging, Marissa and I didn't come to where you live and disturb you or your life. You showed up here at my house. Don't try to tell me how to react when I'm standing in my own house. Now, I've already told you she's not here and the next time you decide to drop by unannounced, don't," Martika chided.

Marissa used her hand to halt her mother's attempt at closing the door to shut her out. She was prepared, knowing that was coming next.

"I know you're raising her, but Lacey is still my daughter and I have a right to see her," Marissa pleaded in a softer voice. Could her mother still be this angry after all the years that had passed? She knew she hadn't done right by Lacey, but she visited when she could.

"Rights? You don't have any rights or at least none that you can use when you come here. You lost those rights the day you decided to choose that crook over your own daughter and your father and I had to take on raising her. She doesn't need you or the drama that comes along with you disrupting her life. I told you to get it together and we can talk about visitation rights. Until then, you can call on the phone at the already approved time. I don't want her seeing you like this. Did you even change after last night's show? Go home and come back when you look better, more decent and most important, call first."

Marissa looked down at herself and used the oversized suit jacket around her shoulders to cover up as much of her exposed skin as she could. She had found the jacket that belonged to Wayne, in the trunk of her car. She knew she still had on the red wig from the night before and her face may have still had signs of the glitter that had covered her body. The jacket did a great job covering up the gold glitter covered mini dress she wore underneath, but her mother already knew what was under it. The jacket had more material than her dress did. She wasn't in the mood for another fight and the last thing she wanted her to know was that she no longer had a place to live other than her car. In one week, her life had completely bottomed out and the only bright spot in her life was her daughter Lacey and she needed to see her. Lacey was her only connection to sanity. A week ago, she had picked up a razor and the unthinkable had crossed her mind. Things I her life hadn't gotten much better and all she needed was to see Lacey's beautiful face and hear her call her mommy. She needed someone who loved her unconditionally.

"Mom, I didn't come here to argue. Since Lacey isn't here, I'll try another time."

"No, you will not!" Martika bellowed. "You'll call like I asked you to do and not drop by when you want to. We're going to church Sunday. Feel free to find some decent clothes and join us in worship. I may let you spend some unscheduled time with Lacey then."

The disgust was evident in every word her mother spoke and each word cut into her like a knife. Her disappointment was obvious, but Lacey was still her daughter and she was also done with people telling her what to do with her life.

"You know I can't do that. Church isn't my thing," she said.

Marissa didn't want to say it, but there was nothing for her behind any church doors. She felt that God had given up on her a long time ago and no longer knew her name.

"It isn't your thing? You can't go to church? Well, that's where we'll be if you want to see Lacey," her mother said matter-of-factly.

Marissa knew where the conversation was heading and it was going to be all about church. That wasn't her cup of tea and she didn't want to hear anything about church or God. Neither had ever done anything for her or she wouldn't be living in her car and working as a stripper in a club. If it wasn't for Wayne throwing her and all of her things out on the street a few nights ago, she would be lower than she was right now. There was no need to tell her mother any of it. All she knew how to do was judge.

Rather than continue to stand on the front porch and be openly disrespected, she turned and began walking back down the steps. She had everything she owned in the world piled up in the back seat of her car and she had hoped seeing Lacey's beautiful face could help take away some of the loneliness she felt. She turned back before her mother closed the door.

"Can you tell Lacey I love her and I'll talk to her soon, please? You know I'm trying my best, momma. I'm trying to make do with what I have," she said walking down the last few steps.

"That's not the best you can do. I'm your mother and I know that. This is not the daughter I raised, living with some man who sells poison to our people on the streets, who has you dancing for money in clubs and showing strange men your body. Only God knows what else you do for money. You think because he bought you some fancy car and has you living in some big ol' fancy apartment makes you something? It doesn't. You gave up on being something the day you left Lacey with us and didn't return."

Marissa stopped walking and turned back around after quickly scanning the block to see if anyone was listening to them. Hearing her mother pass out judgement like the judge and jury hurt her deeply and she did everything in her power to hold back the tears that threatened to fall. She beat up on herself enough every day and she didn't need anyone else to do it, especially her mother.

"I gave Lacey to you because I couldn't have her with me and what was the other option? Put her in the system? I admit I made a lot of bad choices, but the best choice I made was handing her over to you and daddy. I never thought that every time I came around you would throw everything about me back in my face. Maybe if you were more supportive, I would have taken a different route," she said in anger through gritted teeth.

She knew she'd hit a nerve when her mother, who was usually more reserved around neighbors, stepped outside of the house and onto the porch. Today, it seems she didn't care if others saw or heard her chastising her daughter publicly.

"Oh, is that it? I wasn't supportive enough as a mother? I sent you to private school to get the best education and your father and I struggled to do that. You were enrolled in dance classes, gymnastics, two activities where you were at the top of the class along with other activities to keep your mind occupied. We took you to church every Sunday where you sang on

the choir, danced on the children's dance ministry and so many other activities to keep you connected to God, but you turned your back on all of that the minute some slick talking fool smiled at you and threw a few dollars your way. He got you pregnant and didn't have a problem driving you here to drop the baby off and never coming back for her. He's never seen her since the two of you dropped her off as if she was a bag of dirty laundry. Is that doing your best? Yes, your father and I are raising her, but you're her mother and you're supposed to love and care for her. You are supposed to put her before some drug dealing pimp. You think staying with a man like that for all these years is doing your best? Well, I'd hate to see you at your worse or is that what this is right now at the age of twenty-six? Don't blame your father and I for what you've become. You chose this, so look in the mirror when you want to blame someone for how your life turned out."

Marissa was about to counter and get defensive as she always did which often turned into a shouting match, but before she could come back with a retort, her mother turned and went back in the house and slammed the door. She guessed that meant the conversation was over.

Her first thought was to go back up and ring the bell again, but decided against it. There was no need to dig a deeper hole for her mother to push her into. She knew she'd messed up and that was something she lived with every day. That revelation was the only reason she didn't go running back to Wayne when he threw her out, leaving her to drive around New Jersey with no place to go where he wouldn't be able to find her. This was her life now; a life of loneliness and despair. Could her mother really believe she asked for this?

Walking with her head down and her shoulders slumped, Marissa raced to her car after the unsavory encounter with her mother. She was tired of the nasty back and forth between them whenever she saw her or called on the phone to talk to Lacey. Her mother claimed to be a child of God, yet she has yet to forgive her own daughter even if the choices she made over and over again were terrible ones. They were her choices, good or bad.

Just as she reached the car door, she saw a familiar face jogging toward her. She tried to look away, but couldn't. She had a feeling Raquel had already seen her and even in her long red wig, make-up and night club attire, she was recognizable.

She and Raquel had grown up in this neighborhood and had even attended the same church and schools. At one time, they were closer than most sisters until life took them in two different directions. She remembered the good friendship they once shared and it would be rude of her to act like she didn't see her about to jog her way. She took a second to try and straighten her clothes by pulling the short, mini dress down as far as she could and then realized there was no use. It still wouldn't move down any further than right below her behind. She wanted to rip the red wig from her head, but underneath was an ugly brown stocking cap covering up braids that were weeks old. She'd grown so accustomed to wigs, that she'd begun to ignore her own natural hair. She watched as Raquel, now about a half a block away, lowered her sunglasses and recognized her. Marissa put on a smile, though she felt exposed and embarrassed. It had been a long time since she'd run into anyone from the old neighborhood. To show that she also recognized her, Marissa gave her a little wave along with a little brighter smile. Her smile turned to a frown when Raquel crossed the street in the middle of the block, reached the sidewalk on the other side and ran back the other way. For a second, she thought that perhaps Raquel didn't see her, but when she looked back, put her sunglasses on and turned her head hard to be sure Marissa saw her blatantly ignoring her, she got her answer. Like most of the people she knew from her life before, Raquel shunned her as if she was a leper. Wasn't she now a minister's wife? Church people, she thought and then got in her car. Sometimes they could be the worst of the worst.

One of the reasons she ended up in her current situation was due to the fakeness she encountered in church. Her experience was totally different than she thought it would be after growing up in church and thinking that what she learned in the Bible about loving others as God loved you would be what she would find, but that wasn't the case. They were more judgmental and mean for no reason. Women shunned her because as she grew into a woman, their men started looking at her, not as a young girl, but as a growing, flourishing young woman who was filling out in all the places they liked. That wasn't her fault and she never led anyone on, but still the looks and stares she received turned her away. She didn't find love in the church and what terrified her more was the love she felt like she'd found in the streets. It wasn't until recently that she began questioning every choice she'd ever made.

Marissa sat for a while before starting her car. For the first time in a long time, she didn't have a place to go home to. What was she going to do? She could rent a hotel room for as long as her money would take her and luckily, Wayne hadn't realized that she was taking from his stash whenever he wasn't looking. There were times when he'd have piles and stacks of money laying around on the dresser in their bedroom and she'd take a few hundred here and there and he never noticed. There would be so much money at their place that she knew until he counted it, he didn't know how much he'd brought in. Wayne was like that. As long as he saw a lot of it, he didn't care what the actual count was until it was all counted and packaged up to be taken to one of the storage units where he kept his money. She had quite a few thousand tucked away in a bank account and had about nine thousand in cash on her. Without a job, she needed to be careful what she spent to make it stretch, hoping if the money ran low, she wouldn't resort to going back to the life she needed to escape from.

Her phone rang as she sat wondering what her next move would be. She saw Crystal's picture appear on the screen.

"Hello," she answered somberly.

"Delilah, where are you girl? You left the club a few nights ago before I had the chance to talk to you and I thought you were there to dance. Klaus said you were no longer employed at the club and Wayne told him to never let you in again. I saw the bruises on your body that you tried to cover up the last time you danced. What happened and are you alright?" she asked.

"I'm fine. I had to get out of there. Wayne and I are finished and we got into it a little bit. The bruises will heal, but I'm done with him and with that club."

"You can still make some money if you need it. I had a couple of big-ballers who wanted us for a private party after the club. I looked all over for you. They requested you especially, like most of the men who come in there do. They paid big money and I was hoping you would finally jump on the band wagon for some of the more exclusive parties. It would work out great now that Wayne isn't hovering."

"Crystal, you know I'm not about that. I dance and that's pretty much it. The old me was stupid and now,

I don't go for that borderline prostitution. I don't judge any of the girls, but that's not me anymore."

"Girl, that's what we all said at one time or another. Is it because of Wayne? He wouldn't care. It's not like he didn't meet you in the clubs. Plus, I heard things weren't going all that well with him anyway. Chauncy saw him at a spot in New Jersey last night with some young girl all over him. I hear he's already talking about her being the next big thing, even bigger than you – that's according to him, not me."

Marissa already knew about her. That same girl had been the cause of the fight she had with Wayne right before he threw her out of the condo they shared. It was that same girl who helped him and some of his friends throw all of her clothes and other items out on the street. As she picked up her things that were strewn about, she could hear them laughing, calling her names and daring her to step foot on the property ever again. Wayne told her to not even thing about taking her car since he'd bought it, but the minute she'd scooped up her belongings, she ran for the car before his goons could catch up to her.

"Wayne is a grown man and he can do who or whatever he wants. Any new woman will soon learn like I did just how brutal he can be and if they want to put up with it, good for them. I may not be perfect, but I'm no man's punching bag."

"So, he did put those bruises on you?" Crystal asked.

Marissa didn't want to talk about her personal life. She didn't mind befriending some of the girls at the club, but she didn't share a lot of personal business with them and now wasn't a time to start.

"I'm fine Crystal."

"Okay, well what are you going to do? Chauncy knows of some other clubs that you could dance at that Wayne won't have a connection to. I can get some leads for you. Where are you staying? You can stay with us for a while if you need a bed to lay your head on. I'm sure Chauncy wouldn't mind."

Marissa already knew he wouldn't mind. More than once, Chauncy had made a play for her without Crystal knowing about it and she had a feeling if she stayed with them, she'd be going from the fire into the frying pan. The last thing she needed was to be placed in a compromising position. There would be no telling what Chauncy would want as payment for a place to lay her head. She was finally away from Wayne and for once she had the strength to not go back.

"I'm good. I have a place to stay and I already have a new spot to dance at that Wayne knows nothing about," she sort-of lied.

"Okay, girl. I was just checking on you."

"I appreciate it, but I'm fine. Really I am."

Marissa tried to make her voice sound cheery and get the conversation over with.

"Well, let me know where you're at now and I'll come by and check out your set. Maybe you can put in a word for me and get me a few nights. You know we make a great team!" Crystal said, jubilantly.

Marissa shrugged. They didn't make a good team. She helped Crystal make a lot of money by the men 'Delilah' brought in each night.

"I'll call you next week. I'm off this weekend, so next week will be better," she lied again.

"Sounds like a plan. I know what a bully Wayne can be, but you know he really loves you. Give him some time and I'm sure he'll take you back. Chauncy and I go through that all the time and I'm still here. No one walks away from the lifestyle these guys provide for us. We're the girlfriends and not just more of these girls that make money for them, so that makes us special, right?" Crystal asked.

Marissa held her phone out and looked at it. That was the dumbest comment she'd ever heard. No need in pissing Crystal off or hurting her feelings by bringing reality into her world.

"I'll call you, okay?" she said and disconnected the call before Crystal could respond or jump into another conversation.

She and Crystal had the same ailment – they didn't know when something was bad for them and men like Wayne and Chauncy were the worst. She had a connection to Wayne that Crystal didn't have to Chauncy; they shared a daughter that Wayne cared nothing about and she was happy about that. Lacey's life didn't need that kind of disruption to know that she had a pimping, drug dealer for a father. Having a pole swinging exotic dancer as a mother wasn't much better, but at least she loved Lacey. Wayne refused to even say her name.

She hadn't totally lied to Crystal about dancing. In the few days that she'd been on her own, a dancer she trusted gave her the contact information for another club where she could become someone new and at least keep money in her pocket.

After putting her phone back in her purse, she started her car up and was about to pull out of the parking space when she saw her father's car pass her, heading towards their house. She made a U-turn and followed him back down the block. She wanted to get out and hug and kiss Lacey, who at six years old, was her mini-me. Before acting on impulse, she decided her mother was right; it wasn't the right time or place for a reunion with her. It had been six months since she'd last seen Lacey in person, though they had seen each other over the phone a few times. She may not be an active part of Lacey's life, but she was still her mother. She may not be the kind of mother a child would be proud to have, but she was her mother and one day, she hoped she could be a person her daughter would be proud to call mommy.

She drove by the house slowly as her father got out and then opened the car door to let Lacey out. Seeing her brought tears to her eyes. Lacey was getting bigger and prettier with each passing day. She'd already grown in height since the last time she'd seen her. Her long, thick black hair was pulled up into a tight bun, most likely for ballet. She had a bright pink hair ribbon around it, tied into a pretty bow in the front. She was still in her dancing leotard and tutu and was as cute as a button. She wanted to see her but she didn't want to scare her if she showed up dressed in stripper attire. What was she thinking about showing up dressed like this? The only thought on her mind was finding a face that loved her and not the monster she saw when she looked at Wayne, especially the day he'd thrown her out.

A few weeks after her encounter with Klaus, she'd overheard Wayne making a plan to make more money off of her by 'loaning' her out for top dollar. He didn't realize she was standing on the other side of the door where he and other men negotiated what Wayne felt was top dollar.

Two weeks later, he finally brought up the subject and it turned into a huge fight when she pointedly told him she wasn't a prostitute. Of course, he resorted to his retort about how he'd rescued her from her dismal life at home with her parents. She couldn't believe he thought he'd actually rescued her after what she allowed him to put her through.

The fight started as it had so many times before, but this time, she stood up to him, something he hated. She told him what she thought about him and all the other women, including the one who was at their place standing before her who she doubted was even of legal age. The moment he'd hit her like she was a man, she knew things were over. As the fight grew bigger and louder, the front door opened and in walked his thugs, whom he considered muscle for him.

Emboldened with rage, Wayne unleashed a barrage of expletives and other words uncharacteristic of names she never wanted to be called again. The rest was a blur until she found herself out on the street with her belongings being thrown out with her. She started to cry and then realized, if he wanted her gone, she would be ghost. With her head up high, she picked up her belongings in the midst of yelling and catcalls, got in her car and sped off, never looking back. The next day, word had gotten back to her that Wayne was looking for her and wanted her back. When she went by the club to get her schedule, Klaus let her know that she wasn't welcomed again until Wayne said so. That was his way of keeping his hold on her even after the way he treated her. She grabbed what was hers and once again, never looked back.

After watching her father and Lacey enter the house, it was time for her to leave. Wiping the tears that had fallen, she turned down the next street and headed out of the neighborhood and headed to New York. The new dance spot was in the city and she hoped beyond Wayne's reach. She was on her own for the first time in a long time. She still wasn't on the right path, but it was her path. She wasn't wanted at home, though something in her wanted to beg her mother to let her in and allow her to stay. She wanted to change her life, but didn't know how to. She was lonely and alone and had no one to give her the love and support she deeply needed. All she needed was a small sign that her mother would forgive and receive her, but that wasn't to be. Back to the streets is where she was headed. The streets loved her more than her mother and as the tears really began to fall and her body heaved from the force of the guttural cries, she sped away from her childhood home as fast as she could. She wasn't wanted, but she knew she would be back. She was as low as anyone could be, but still, her thoughts turned to Lacey and she smiled. She would be back.

7

Roman was counting down the clock that signaled the end of his overnight shift as he drove around the community. For a change, he hadn't received many calls tonight and those that he did receive weren't major issues. The big plus was he didn't have to place anyone in the back of his patrol car. What frustrated him most was how he was unable to shake despair over where his life was heading. His job was still a place of anguish and from where he sat, he wasn't having much of an impact on the streets. He'd struggled over a decision regarding his career that he hoped would put him on a path to really do some good.

He was looking at three days off where he hoped to put in his notice that he would be leaving the force. He knew that some were going to see it as him letting the streets defeat him, but perhaps that's what he needed. There were days that he felt that way. He wasn't seeing a difference on the streets of Philly and he tried hard every day to be a part of a change he longed for. He had a heart for the people, yet the need to do more still tugged at him. He was the kind of cop that wanted to get to know the people on his route and he wanted them to know who he was and what he was about. He never believed he was in position to only police those who were doing wrong – he wanted to be a part of those who were doing good.

He had begun spending more time at the athletic league in his district, lending a helping hand with the programs for youth which included not just athletics, but time spent helping them with homework, computer skills and most importantly and something he was passionate about, reading. Though he hadn't gone off to college, Melanie had and literacy was important to her. She always said getting in touch with children in a positive way could lead to them being a positive force in their own communities. It was being a part of ongoing activities around him that fed his need to be helpful the most. Being a cop could be fulfilling, but he encountered a lot of fellow officers who had a different outlook on their purpose than he did. He spent more time locking up offenders than really helping them. Where he was the cool, level headed cop, there were many who set out on each shift ready to pack the jail cells with people. He wanted to make a difference, something he and Melanie often talked about. The athletic league had been reaching out to him for months about coming on board full-time whenever he was ready, but he knew he couldn't do that and keep his job on the force.

There would be no time for Nina and that would never work. Maybe it was time for him to give up his job as an officer. The streets didn't need him as much as the youth at the center did.

Tonight, he realized, could be one of his last nights on the job. He would put in his notice and spend his last two weeks using up vacation time he had accrued. The streets no longer needed him.

The was two blocks from the station house and he had thirty minutes before the end of his shift and figured he would use it finishing up paperwork to not leave anything undone when he resigned. His thoughts were broken into by his car radio.

"Officer Hale, can you take one last call before the end of your shift? There is a woman reporting a suspicious car parked outside of her house and she's scared. She's an older woman who lives alone and she said the car has been sitting out there all night and it looks to her like there's a person in it. It's probably nothing, but I figured since it's on your way back to the station, you wouldn't mind checking into it. A second car is also on the way," the dispatcher said.

"Ten-four. I'm on my way," he replied, turning his patrol car around.

Finding no need for a siren at six in the morning, he approached the block and noticed the black car sitting at the end of the block. Looking at the house with the address of the woman who called, he saw an older woman in the window who pointed at the car for him. He gave her a wave that he had it under control. Driving by the car to check it out, he could see that the driver's side seat was laid all the way back and there appeared to be a person inside, asleep. Pulling ahead of the car, he acknowledged the other patrol car as it pulled up beside him as he was getting out.

"What's up Roman?"

"Not much," he said to Dave, another officer.

"What do we have here?" Dave asked.

"I don't think it's much. Looks like someone is asleep in the car. The woman who lives in the house in front of the car called in a complaint of a strange car being outside of her house all night. She was worried when she realized a person was inside of it the whole night. Let's check it out," he said.

Roman walked ahead of Dave with his hand on his weapon, just in case. He knew they couldn't take a chance on thinking it was nothing when it could turn out to be something. As Dave walked to the passenger side, he walked up to the driver's side and got a closer look. Inside, there was a woman asleep with a blanket covering her. He also noticed the back seat of the car was full with a lot of personal items and quite a few big trash bags, most likely full of her belongings. He wasn't sure what to make of the situation and after signaling Dave, he knocked on the window. At first, the woman didn't move. He waited and knocked again, this time a little harder and that finally woke her up. Once she noticed the two officer's he watched as she reached for the automatic button and lowered the window.

"Good morning, officer," she said.

"Good morning. Are you alright in there?" Roman asked as Dave used his flashlight to look around the inside of the car.

"Oh, yes. I'm sorry, I fell asleep."

"We received a call from one of the neighbors. Have you been drinking? Why are you asleep here?" he asked.

"No, I haven't been drinking, I was only sleeping."

"Can I see your license and registration, please?" he asked.

"Sure. I'm sorry. I wasn't disturbing anyone."

Roman waited for her to pull out her two forms of identification as he took a closer look at her, the car and the items in the back.

"You can hand everything to the officer on the other side of the car," he said. "What's your name?" he asked.

"It's Marissa. Marissa Ballard."

"Ms. Ballard, can you step out of the car for a minute, please?" Roman asked and stepped back, still with his hand on his service weapon.

"Yes." Marissa opened the car door and stepped out. She was glad she'd changed out of her clothes after working at the club the night before. She had put on a black velour sweat suit, great for the September weather. She'd also put on her favorite pair of black and red Nike sneakers. She was glad to have taken a shower at the club the night before, washed her make-up off and washed and shampooed her hair before pulling it up into a loose ponytail.

After she exited the car, Roman was able to get an even better look at her. His immediate perusal was to check for any signs that she had been drinking or perhaps doing drugs – he didn't see any.

"What are you doing out here this early in the morning asleep in your car?" he asked.

"I drove in from New York, not really with a plan and it was late. I pulled over in a spot that I thought was out of the way in order to get some sleep," she explained.

"She's good," Dave said walking back over to them. "No warrants and the car is in her name, no tickets or anything."

Dave handed her identification to Roman who checked it out before handing it back to her.

"That's good to know. It looks like Ms. Ballard was driving and pulled over when she got tired. Where were you driving to? It looks like you live in New Jersey," Roman said.

"I do or I did. Officially, I guess I still do. Right now, I'm in between locations. I have family here in Philadelphia."

"Why didn't you go to them when you arrived?" he asked.

Marissa didn't know what to say without telling her

entire life story.

"It's pretty complicated," she said softly and looked away from his glare to look down at the ground.

"Roman, are you good here if I take off? This doesn't seem like a big issue," Dave said.

"Yeah, go ahead. I'll be right behind you in a few."

Roman watched as Dave headed toward his car, hopped in and drove off. He turned his attention back to the woman.

"Ms. Ballard it's dangerous to sleep in your car. The neighbors were concerned when it appeared someone was in the car and possibly watching their homes."

"I'm sorry, I wasn't doing that. I really was sleeping," she explained.

"I can see that. Why is that? Why are you sleeping in your car?"

Marissa stumbled over her words.

"I don't have any place to go," she admitted. That was the first time she'd said the words out loud.

Roman couldn't believe what he was hearing. Here stood a beautiful young woman, driving what he knew was a seventy-five-thousand-dollar car and yet she had no place to go? Her story wasn't adding up.

"Ms. Ballard, it's not a crime to sleep in your car, but you're going to have to move off of this street and hopefully to a friend's house, a hotel or perhaps home?"

Marissa looked down at the ground again. She didn't want to explain that she was living in her car and had driven to Philadelphia because she wanted to be closer to her daughter.

"I'll just get moving. I didn't mean to cause anyone to be afraid."

"Well, in this day and age, people are suspicious of everyone," he said laughing.

Marissa looked up at him and smiled for the first time in days.

"I guess it would look strange to someone else and I didn't think of that."

"It's dangerous to just be out here. I know of a few places you could go if you don't have a place to be. You need to get off of the streets. You're making yourself a target."

"I know and I will. I used to live here, right around the corner actually, before I moved to New Jersey some years back. I'm back now and I guess I didn't have a plan in place for coming back."

"You said you had family, so why not go to them?" he asked again.

Roman didn't mean to pry, but surprising himself, he found her intriguing. It had nothing to do with how beautiful she was because it had been a long time since he'd seen a woman this gorgeous. There was something about her that drew him in. He felt a strong need to help her. She wasn't some damsel in distress, but she was a woman who looked like she had seen better days by the way she kept looking at the ground and not up at him.

"That's a long story. Let's just say right now, I'm on my own. Look, I'm sorry and I didn't mean to cause any trouble, I promise. Is it okay if I leave now?" she asked.

Roman handed her the identification back and nodded that she could leave.

"Stay safe Ms. Ballard and please no more sleeping in your car. There are places that can help you."

Marissa didn't respond. She nodded her head and got in her car. Without wasting any time, she put her car in drive and pulled away from the curb, leaving the officer standing in the street watching her drive away. She finally exhaled thinking the encounter went better than she thought. She didn't know if she'd end up being locked up or in some other kind of trouble. The car was in her name, but there were times that Wayne used it and he could have been up to no good in it. She'd had run-ins with other police over the years and not once has any ever been as nice as the one officer had been with her. He actually sounded calm and caring as if he was truly concerned about her welfare and not just trying to get her to move so that he could go home. She was thankful that he showed compassion, but like she told him, she didn't have a place to go.

After trying her hand at dancing again a few weeks ago after her last visit home when she had that awful talk with her mother, she was back again. After returning first to New Jersey, drawn back to the only life she'd known, she drove around knowing someone would notice her in her flashy car. Within hours, she was being followed around by some of Wayne's men and knew that she was in danger of being accosted. She should have gone straight to New York for the dancing gig that she was able to line up to keep money flowing, but no, she was a glutton for punishment. She wanted to see if Wayne really had moved on with that young girl without even caring where she was. She finally left and headed for New York.

Things had been going well for a few weeks in New York and she'd been able to get a room at a motel until she decided what her moves were going to be. Her last night in New York, she was heading out for her set on the main club stage when she looked out through the curtain and saw Wayne sitting at the table directly in front of the stage. Her heart raced as she tried to figure out a way to get out of the club. There was no way she'd go out on stage with him there. Somehow, he'd found out where she was and was waiting for her. While the crowd waited, she faked leaving something in her dressing room and raced back to it. Grabbing her clothes without changing out of the red sheer outfit that showed her silver thong and six-inch silver stilettos, she made a run for the back door, ran three blocks to the motel where she'd been staying and never looked back. She raced into the room she'd been renting by the day, quickly grabbed up everything she owned, tossed it into the backseat and trunk of her car and while making sure she didn't see anyone that would make her believe Wayne was following her, she jumped in her car and drove until she reached Philadelphia. It may have been a place where she wasn't wanted, but it was the only place she felt safe.

After not knowing where to go, she pulled over a few blocks from her parent's house into a space she thought was dark enough to hide her presence and she grabbed a blanket, wrapped it around her and after making sure the doors were locked, she attempted to get some sleep until the officer knocked on the window.

Now, driving through traffic, she didn't know where she was going. Surprising herself, she looked out of the window as she passed by the church that she'd belonged to with her family until she packed up and left. The church loomed high above her like a large dark and gloomy castle from a scary movie. The building held a lot of memories for her, more bad than good. She'd been through a lot at that church and out on the streets and where was this infinite God who protected His people? Why didn't she feel welcomed and safe in His church? The things that happened to her in the church would haunt her forever.

Silently, she had prayed to a God she thought existed only because she had been told all she had to do was ask and she would receive. Well, she had practically been begging the past few months for God to help her and yet, here she was with no place to go.

She didn't have church or family, so what was left for her?

As she drove on with the church in her rearview mirror, she tried to find the words to pray to see if a God she'd heard so much about could hear her and know her pain, but the words wouldn't come. She didn't know why she would have to beg God for help when if He was this powerful being, He would know she needed His helping hand. If He was real, why was she all alone in the world?

8

Roman walked into the station house locker room still unable to get the woman who was sleeping in her car out of his mind. After she pulled off and drove out of sight, he sat in his car and thought about the encounter. What was it about her that he couldn't seem to shake? She was beautiful? Yes. She was helpless? Yes. She seemed vulnerable and in need of a friend? Yes, to that, too. What disturbed him the most was the loneliness he saw in her eyes when she looked up at him. His heart sank wondering what could have a young woman so down that her eyes were the saddest he'd ever seen.

He sat down in front of his locker, still puzzled as officers buzzed around him.

"Roman, how did that situation turn out this morning with that woman in the car after I left?"

Roman turned to see Dave enter the locker room.

"No harm was done. She got in her car and drove off," he said.

"That was something, huh? A beautiful woman like that sleeping in her car. I bet she was on drugs or hiding from a pimp or something. You should have brought her in and let her sleep it off in a cell. People can't just decide to sleep in cars all over the city. There are real crimes going on in the streets and we had to waste our time with her. You should have locked her up for stupidity!" Dave hollered.

"Really, Dave? She was a woman in need and there are a lot of people living in their cars and on the streets and those people are just like you and me," he said.

Roman was disturbed how cops like Dave wore the uniform and had no heart. Dave was known for using more force than was necessary and getting into confrontations with people just to throw his weight around. Cops like him gave good cops a bad name.

"Man, that girl was driving around in a car I wish I could afford and yet she's living in it? Please, she was up to no good. She probably had a partner in crime who spotted us and made a run for it. She could have been the getaway driver in a home invasion or something," he said.

Roman turned fully around in his direction.

"Seriously? You think she was sitting in her car waiting for someone to come back after burglarizing a house. Was there a call we didn't know about regarding a burglary last night? Not everyone is up to no good, you know."

Dave dismissed him.

"Yeah, whatever. I forgot, you're the deacon cop

who sees the good in everyone."

Roman hated when officers tried to make a joke out of his position in church and how he walked the walked and talked the talk. His faith was important to him and got him through a tough time in his life. He wasn't one to allow it to be used as fodder in the locker room.

"My being a deacon in my church has nothing to do with my believing that not everyone is out to commit a crime."

"Well, she was lucky she encountered you before me because I would have brought her in and at least kept her overnight until she explained what she was really doing sitting in a fancy car on the street. She looked like a sore thumb and she was a little nervous if you ask me. I guess you'll miss being the good cop once you resign, huh? What will the good people of Philadelphia do then?" Dave asked. He didn't give Roman a chance to respond as he grabbed his duffle bag from his locker and headed for the showers. Roman kept his response to himself and thought about Dave's passing words.

During a conversation a few nights ago, he'd shared with Dave that he was planning on resigning and doing something else with his life. He was tired of the heartache and misery found on the streets. Dave didn't believe him and now he was beginning to doubt himself. What if the woman sleeping in her car had encountered Dave and not him? What would have happened to her? She didn't need a night in jail. She looked like she needed someone to give her a break and he did. He only hoped she found someplace safe to get some rest.

He'd driven off wondering why she didn't go to her family if she was without a place to sleep. A woman alone and on the streets should have family or friends to take her in. He didn't know her circumstance, but ever since he came across her, he hadn't been able to shake how sad she looked. It was because of people like her that he stayed on the force as long as he had. He wouldn't want the people of Philadelphia to only be exposed to cops like Dave who spent more time having internal affairs investigate one complaint or another against him. Dave had a history of excessive force and unwelcomed attention on females he came across during his shift. The streets needed more cops like him and less like Dave. Is this really a good time to leave? He couldn't help but think about the woman and what her fate would have been if Dave had gotten to the call first.

"Roman? Captain Miller wants to see you."

Roman looked up as an officer called his name.

"I'll be right there," he said. No doubt, his captain wanted to know if he was still planning to leave the force. He was told to think about it and was told that good cops like him who had a heart for the people were hard to find and communities needed men like him. Grabbing what he needed from his locker, he headed toward his captain's office.

Before he got the chance to knock, he waved him in while he finished up a phone call. Roman took the seat across from him and waited until the call ended.

"I think today was the day for your decision. What did you decide? Am I losing one of the best cops I have around here?" Captain Miller said.

Roman stared at him, ready to blurt out the decision he was sure was the right one until a few hours ago. His encounter with the woman sleeping in her car was imprinted on him. Along with that, the short chat he had with Dave poked at him, too. What played in his mind over and over again is what would have happened to the woman if Dave had been in his place last night? He couldn't leave the streets to cops like Dave without an alternative like him. He couldn't rescue everyone he came across, but if he could help a few because he wore a uniform, he should do it.

"I'm hanging around. I've been having a real pity party for myself lately and it got the best of me. I've been praying about it and until a few hours ago, I was sure it was time for me to leave, but not now."

Roman watched as his captain sat up straight in his chair.

"Something happen out there I should know about?" Captain Miller said.

Roman thought about the woman and knew that he could tell his captain anything. He was not only the captain, but they had become good friends over the years. He started out as a father figure, but that turned into a great friendship, one he had come to depend on especially after the loss of his wife. His captain and his wife were good to him during everything that came after Melanie's death. His wife had even taken Nina home with them for a few days to allow him to plan out the services for Melanie and deal with the aftermath.

"Nothing major. I ran into this woman," he said.

"A woman? Was she pretty and what does she have to do with you being a cop after today?"

"Captain," Roman said and then he stopped.

"You're off the clock and so am I. When we're not working, it's Owen," he said.

Roman smiled, forgetting that when they weren't on the clock, he hated being called captain. He smiled.

"Okay, Owen. For starters, yes, she was pretty, but that doesn't have anything to do with anything. She made me realize I am needed on the streets now more than ever, especially if the alternative is leaving the people of Philly in the hands of cops like Dave. He's a friend and I respect his thoughts because they are his, but they're not always the most logical."

Owen laughed.

"Dave is definitely a special case and I'm hoping a lot of who you are will rub off on him. I need you around longer and I'm glad you're staying. Now, who was this woman? Something in the way you're thinking about her while you're talking has me intrigued."

Roman smiled again.

"Don't be too intrigued. She was a call and living in her car. There was something about her, though. I don't know, I could be thinking about it too hard. Anyway, I'm getting out of here. For a change, I get to go home and sleep the day away or at least until I have to pick Nina up from cheerleader practice later today after school and take her to story time. I'm still going to devote a little more time to the athletic league because they need the help, but I'm not going to do it full-time."

Roman stood to leave.

"I'm really glad you're staying around and I know Melanie would be glad you are, too. I know this is a thankless job and sometimes you feel like you can't make a difference, but just because you can't touch that change to know it actually happened, I believe you've had a major impact and staying around is good for the people and good for you."

"I appreciate that, captain."

"Good, then next week, Sadie and I are having some friends over the house and don't try saying no when I already know you're off that weekend. See the perks of being friends with your captain?"

Roman shook his head. As long as it's Saturday. After the first three services at church, my pastor is preaching at another church and I'm on detail that evening."

"You and that church. Do you even have a life outside of this place and that church?"

"It's because of that place that I have a life outside of this place. Don't start on me about church. I get enough of that from the guys around here. I don't know what you people have against going to church. You should try it on days besides Mother's Day and Easter," he quipped.

"Yeah, yeah. Next Saturday and feel free to bring a date."

"A date? I'm not dating, so there will be no date."

"Not dating? Aw, man. You need a woman to rescue you from this boring, stoic life you're choosing to live."

Roman opened the door to head out.

"Thanks for being patient with me about this. I got it together now," Roman said and closed the office door behind him as he left.

Walking out of the station house, his mind was still on the woman in the car as he headed toward his truck. He couldn't shake the idea that he wished he could have had more time to talk to her and wondered if there would be a circumstance where he would see her again. He really wanted to.

**

Marissa kept at least two cars between her and her father's car as she followed him and Lacey from their house through the streets. She tried her best to keep her eye on them and not lose them.

In the light of day, after her night of sleeping in her

car and then driving the streets aimlessly, she was able to find a place at a local gym to shower and change her clothes after slipping one of the guys behind the counter some money to let her in for a few hours to clean up. She headed back to her parent's house, not to stir up trouble, but hoping to get a look at Lacey for more than a few seconds. What she didn't want was another encounter with her mother, but she needed to see her daughter. When she pulled onto their street, like the day before, she saw her father driving down the street and when she stretched her neck, she saw Lacey in the back seat leaning down most likely reading. She may be a sad excuse for a mother, but each month, she mailed several books to Lacey and when they got the chance to talk, Lacey would tell her all about the stories she read.

Deciding to follow them to see if they were going to a place in public where she could get a good look at Lacey, she stayed behind them until he pulled up to a park a few blocks away. She smiled when Lacey jumped out of the car and ran across the field to what looked like a cheerleader practice. She didn't know her parents had signed Lacey up to be a cheerleader, something she had also done as a young girl. She waited until her father got out of the car and walked to sit on the bench across from the group of girls, other parents and coaches had gathered for practice before pulling into a parking space. She didn't want to be spotted, but she didn't want to drive away. She wanted to see Lacey at practice and cheer her on as a parent even if she could only do it from a distance. Watching her sit on the ground in a circle with the other little girls reminded her of how much she was missing out on her daughter's life. She was supposed to be the parent with the other mothers, but instead, she was behaving like some type of stalker, watching, but doing so in secret looking through the opening in her steering wheel.

She sat back and watched as practice began and she inwardly cheered and found herself clapping when Lacey did one move or another, showing how flexible she was and how much she loved cheering. Memories flooded back to a time when she enjoyed cheerleading and dancing as a girl. Even back then, her father would take her to practices because her mother was always too busy to take part in any of the activities she'd signed her up for.

After an hour of watching Lacey practice, once the crowd broke up, she was about to pull off before her father spotted her when she saw Lacey and a lot of the other girls' head toward a grassy area where others were gathering. Though practice was over, something else was starting.

"Ready for story time?" a woman asked as she joined the girls in the circle.

Cheerleading and story time? What kind of day was this? She loved Lacey's life.

Instead of leaving, Marissa sat back in her car and

continued watching Lacey. If this was all she as going to get, she was here for it.

**

"Daddy, can I sit with my friends for story time?" Nina asked running up to Roman after practice.

Roman looked where Nina pointed and saw familiar faces as he waved to other parents who had remained after the cheerleading practice. He'd shown up just as rehearsal was ending and after spotting his mother, they'd talked for a few seconds before he thanked her for helping out with Nina. He told her he was off for a few days and was planning to spend some quality time with Nina knowing his schedule lately had been hectic.

"Sure. I'll be right here when it's over."

Roman relaxed back in his folding chair as he watched the kids gather around the woman who was about to begin story time.

The cop in him had him doing a quick check of everything happening in the park. As he scanned around just as the woman from the library began, he noticed a familiar car sitting at the curb watching the crowd. He remembered the car that he'd pulled up to just before his shift had ended and inside, he found a woman sleeping. There was no doubt in his mind it was the same car. He wondered what she was doing at the park. He could see her slouched down in the driver's seat watching the girls barely able to see a suspicious yet cautious look on her face while at the same time, he sensed an innocence about her that he'd picked up on the night before. Standing and walking the long way around the parking lot, he came up to the side of the car, just as he'd done the night before. This time, the window was rolled down a little as he walked up to the passenger side of the car without being noticed. He knocked, startling her as she turned and looked up at him totally shocked.

"Hello?" he said and saw recognition on her face.

"Yes?" she said putting the key in the ignition in order to lower the window more.

"Do you remember me? I'm the officer from this morning," he said.

"Oh, right."

"It's strange to run into you again. I saw you watching the kids over there at the park. Do you have a child over there?" he asked.

"Well, sort of."

"Sort of? What does it mean to sort of have a child?" he asked.

"Well, I have a daughter and she's over there with my father."

"You plan to join them or are you going to watch them from a distance?" he asked.

"They don't know that I'm here."

"I'm not here on official police business. It's my day off and I'm here with my daughter. I saw you and again, you looked a little out of place. Are you sure you're okay?" He looked in the back of her car and it was still full with her belongings. "You didn't find a place to stay?" he asked.

Marissa looked down at her hands, ashamed of her situation, but for now this is what it is. There was no need to lie about her current state of affairs.

"I am and no I didn't. It's not against the law to live in your car," she said boldly.

"I didn't say it was against the law. If you have a father and daughter over there enjoying story time, why wouldn't you want them to know you're here and why would you be living in your car?" he asked. "I don't mean to pry, really I don't. I'm concerned for you."

"Why would you be concerned for me? You don't even know me," she said.

"I don't have to know you to be concerned. I'm not a police officer because there wasn't another career for me. I'm one because I genuinely care about people and if you're living in your car, I'm concerned about you."

"Yeah, well it beats a shelter. Those places are dangerous for anyone, especially a woman," she said.

"You can't stay with your father? Where does your daughter live? Tell me she's not living in this car with you?" he said.

"No, she lives with my parents here in Philadelphia. I haven't seen her in a while and I wanted to get a look at her. I thought I would see him taking her to dance class after school, but instead, they came here to the park. I sort of followed them here. I'm not doing anything wrong," she said defensively.

"No, you're not and like I said, I am merely concerned for you. You are driving around in this very expensive car, yet you don't have a place to live and you're secretly watching your daughter in a crowd while you're slouched down in your car. I'm telling you any other officer would be trying to find a reason to arrest you for something. It's dangerous being out here on the streets of Philly."

"For now, I don't have a place to go and I feel safe in my car. I don't want to make a rash decision with the limited funds I already have, so until I do, this is it."

"Do you mind if I offer a suggestion? You don't have to take it, but I know a place you can go and get off the streets. It's a place where no one will judge your situation."

"Why would you help me?" Marissa asked.

"For starters, I'm a police officer and I'm more than just someone who spends my day locking people up and second, I'm a man of God and it's my duty to help when I see that help is needed. Lastly, I would never want to see a woman living in her car when I know a place she can go to have a roof over her head."

Marissa thought about it and wondered if there was an underlying motive to his offer. She'd encountered so called men of God before and the few she had come up against wanted more from an offer of help. She didn't believe in anyone helping a total stranger.

"What is this place?" she asked.

"My mother and her sister run a house for young women who find that they've fallen on hard times. My aunt lives at the house and my mother is there during the day between that house and the other three they run. You would usually need to go through the system to get a space, but with a recommendation from me, my aunt would have no problem letting you stay. It's a nice house and they help with job searches, computer training as well as counseling services."

"Well, what's in it for you?" she asked.

Roman knew what she meant. He'd heard stories of officers taking advantage of women on the streets, but he wasn't one of those men.

"I know what you're thinking, but I'm not like that. I am offering my help because I care and it's the right thing to do. I'm not out to get anything from you. I don't know what you may have encountered when it comes to me, but trust me, I have no expectations nor am I in need of any returned favors."

Marissa looked him over and wondered what kind of man didn't want something in return for doing a favor. All men wanted something and it usually required being on her knees or flat on her back, neither she'd ever done and never would. She knew a lot of dancers like her who took things to the next level and there were things she'd done that she regretted all for what she thought was for Wayne's love, but nothing like what she hears a lot of girls do especially those who tried giving up dancing and found it hard to survive financially.

"You really want to help me and you're saying I won't owe you anything?" she asked.

"Not everyone wants something from you. If you like, after my daughter finishes, you can follow me to my aunt's place and you can check it out for yourself. If you like it, I'll talk to her. If you don't, please promise me you will find a place and stop sleeping in your car."

"Yes, they usually do. I could tell you some stories, but I'm sure you have some you could tell me with what I'm sure you see every day."

"That I could. Instead of stalking your father and your daughter, why don't you talk to them. I don't know your story, but I bet your daughter would love to see you."

"Well, I'm sure your daughter has a great relationship with her mother and I wish I could say the same for me and my daughter, but I can't."

Roman couldn't find the words the moment a vision of Melanie came to him and what life would have been like for Nina if she had lived. He could picture them getting manicures and going shopping for cute outfits in pink, Nina's favorite color.

"My wife died from cancer when Nina was a baby. She never had the chance to have a relationship with her and I can't tell you how hard that's been for me.

I've tried to fill the gap, but as she gets older, she wonders about her mother and I tell her what I can, but nothing in this world can replace the relationship between a mother and her daughter. I can't tell you what to do, but if you want a relationship with your daughter, don't do it from a distance. You've come this far, from where and what, I don't know, but I get the feeling where you were is worse than where you are right now. If you're looking for a fresh start, I'm offering to help you get it and even if you don't take my advice about your daughter, take the hand I'm offering you and find a way that doesn't have you living in your car. Deal?" he asked.

Marissa thought about it, looking from him to the ground and back up where she saw her daughter clapping and happily bouncing as she listened to story time. She never took the time to be a mother to Lacey and when she decided to pack up shop and come back, her only focus was on finding a way into her daughter's life. She'd messed up and paid the consequences for her bad choices, but Lacey was never a bad choice or decision.

"You're sure about this place?" she asked.

"I'm more than sure."

"Okay. I'll check it out with you. I appreciate the offer."

"Do you want to go over and say hello to your father and your daughter?" he asked.

Marissa started to say she did and then thought

about it.

"I'm going to wait. I need to deal with my own life before I can approach Lacey and explain to her where I've been. Thank you for helping me. You know, I've done some bad things. Are you sure you want to help me? If you knew what the last six or seven years of my life were like, you may second guess helping me. I may not be the kind of person you want to help."

Marissa held her head in shame even though Roman couldn't know what she was talking about. Shame kept her from her daughter all these years and it was still holding her hostage.

"None of us are without sin, but we don't have to walk around in shame. Whatever you've done doesn't matter in your future. What does matter is what you do from this point on."

"Who are you?" Marissa asked.

"What?"

"I've never met anyone who talks like you do. Are you always this optimistic? Are you one of those people who sees the good in everyone?"

"I am or at least I try to be. I don't know you and I see good in you."

"Even when I don't see it in myself?" she asked.

"Yes. Even when you don't see it in yourself." Roman extended his hand to her through the car window. "I am officer Roman Hale, but I'm hoping you'll call me Roman," he added.

"Roman it is and please, call me Marissa."

9

Marissa drove her car, following closely behind Roman and his daughter Nina. After the story time hour, she'd cowered away in her car, slumping down so that she couldn't be seen by her father and Lacey.

As they drove through the streets of Philly, she looked at spots she remembered from years ago and even saw the fast food spot where she had first encountered Wayne and all of his flash and flair. The fact that he took an immediate interest in her at eighteen fascinated her. He'd said all of the right things, pushed all of the right buttons and told her that her beauty and body could take her a long way. She believed him and fell for every line he'd dished out. That was the beginning of her downfall and now, she was homeless, a situation she never thought she would find herself in.

Her thoughts turned to the policeman she was now following. Usually, a man offering her anything came with strings, but when he said he was helping her without looking for anything in return, she trusted him. Unlike her usual terrible choices, something came over her that told her she could trust this man and so she did. This wasn't like the Wayne situation from years ago. Something deep inside of her told her that he was as genuine as they came. He didn't have to help her at all and he definitely didn't have to be nice to her. She wanted to say thanks, but no thanks to his offer of help, but if she were really going to start working on a plan, she had to get off of the street and out of living in her car. The weather would soon turn cold and then where would she be?

After making a few left and then right turns, they pulled in front of a beautiful, large white house with more windows in a house than she'd ever seen. It seemed more like a mansion and the way it stood alone, made her think of old black and white movies with creepy large houses, though this one seemed inviting. The grass was masterfully maintained and the paint looked fresh and new. There was a wooden porch with five steps that led up to it which wrapped around the entire house. There were planters filled with flowers all around the deck and she figured the house must have six or seven bedrooms. It was beautiful.

She parked her car and got out.

"This is your aunt's place?" she asked, amazed. "It's beautiful."

"It is. She and my mother purchased it a few years ago specifically to help women and children in need.

My aunt Vi lives here to oversee the day to day operations. My mother handles the books and all of the ordering of supplies along with dealing with the paperwork for the funding provided by the state. They have helped hundreds of women over the past four years that the house has been open and operating," he explained.

"That's amazing. They do this because they want to?" she asked.

Roman smiled at her.

"Yes, they do. My mother and her sister have always had a heart to help other women. They lost a sister to domestic violence many years ago and have always vowed to help women in need. This is their fourth house and the largest. The city of Philadelphia is grateful for all that they've done. Come on inside and I'll introduce you to my aunt."

Roman opened the back door of his car and a little girl who could have been his twin stepped out.

"Nina, say hello to Ms. Marissa."

"Hello."

"Hello, Nina. You sure are beautiful."

"Thank you," Nina said and grabbed onto Roman's hand.

"Daddy, she's pretty," she said.

"Yes, she is. We're going to introduce her to Aunt Vi."

"Can I go out back to the swings?" Nina asked as she jumped from one leg to the other with excitement.

"Okay, but go inside and say hello first before you run out there. We're not going to be here for long, so don't get comfortable and no whining when we have to leave."

"Okay," Nina said, running ahead of them into the house.

"She's beautiful and a ball of energy I see," Marissa acknowledged.

"That she is and she is my pride and joy. That little girl gives me life!" he shouted. "Come on, let's go find my aunt," Roman said walking ahead of her into the house.

"Hey, Aunt Vi! You here?" Roman called out the minute he and Marissa walked into the house. If his aunt wasn't already in the front room, she probably followed Nina to the backyard.

"In the kitchen!"

"I should have known she would be in the kitchen. I smell something good cooking," Roman said and headed that way with Marissa following close behind.

The minute Vi spotted them, she walked over and gave him a hearty hug.

"Always good to see you, Roman and who do we have here?"

"This is Marissa and she needs a place to stay. Do you have any room here or at one of the other houses? I was going to call mom, but I figured I would start here first. You know how much I love this house," he said.

"Well, you should since most of the restorations were done by you and your friends. Hello, Marissa. Everyone calls me Aunt Vi even if I'm not their aunt and you can, too," she said.

"Thank you, Aunt Vi. This house is beautiful. I thought the outside was lovely and then when we came inside and I got a quick glance at the large main room and this big beautiful kitchen."

"Thank you. I like to make sure the women and children feel like they are at home. How do you know Roman?" she asked as they stood looking each other over.

Marissa didn't know what to say and looked to Roman for help.

"She's down on her luck and I encountered her during my shift and then again at the park today, which means bringing her to meet you was in the cards. Do you have room?" he asked again.

Vi looked at Roman as if to say he shouldn't even have to ask.

"Of course, I do. Let's all have a seat. I've got some fresh rolls from scratch coming out of the oven and we can chow down on a few while we talk. Roman, get the tea out and you can show Marissa where the glasses and plates are."

"Is there apple butter?" he asked.

"I keep it on hand for times like this when you drop by. You must have known I was making rolls. Take a few home with you and Nina when you leave. How's she doing in school?"

"She's doing good. The school year just started last month and so far, she's doing as remarkable as ever. Thankfully, she loves school."

"That's what I like to hear. My precious is growing like a weed. I caught a glimpse of those long legs as she ran out back."

"I know. Sherry or mom will take her shopping for some new things before the weather changes."

As they sat around the table, Marissa couldn't remember a time when she'd felt this comfortable. The banter between aunt and nephew was entertaining and the love was obvious. There was no one judging anything and her stomach growled at the smell and sight of those homemade rolls. She didn't realize how hungry she was.

"These smell delicious," she said.

"You can have as many as you like, but save some room for dinner. Everyone will be piling back in here in an hour and tonight I've made pot roast with little potatoes and carrots, fresh collard greens, my famous corn pudding, braised carrots and I'm planning on frying chicken in the deep fryer out back. These rolls will top off the meal and I've made several dozen," she said.

"Several dozen, Aunt Vi? Really?" Roman asked.

"Yes. I was going to call you stop by and get some and then drop some off with your mom and dad. Sherry called twice last week to ask when I would be making some, so make sure you take her at least half a dozen."

"I'm invited for dinner?" Marissa asked.

"Child, you'll be living here and everyone gets three meals a day. If you get hungry at other times, there is always plenty of food for you to fend for yourself. There are some rules of the house. You have to keep your room cleaned and everyone pitches in with other house cleaning as needed. You're in luck because I actually have two empty bedrooms and you get one to yourself. I would claim that one as soon as we're finished in case Roman comes back with someone else. He refers a lot of women and some with children and we help them all either by giving them a place to stay here or at one of our other houses."

"What does all of this cost? I have some money, but I don't have a job yet," Marissa said as she bit into one of the rolls and moaned, ashamed that she had. She'd never tasted anything so deliciously sweet before and the apple butter added to the delightful taste. She was about to apologize when Roman laughed at her.

"That's the reaction everyone has every time they eat one of her rolls. I keep telling her one day we need to open up a bakery."

"Who has time to run a bakery?" Aunt Vi said. "Now, in response to your question, staying here doesn't cost you a thing other than helping with the upkeep. We will help you with any job training you'll need to help you get back up on your feet and there are no questions asked. There is counseling you'll have to do which is required of all residents and that's to make sure you're doing okay with your current circumstance. There is a job center a few blocks away that you can walk to if you don't have transportation."

"Oh, I have a car."

"Good. You can also help with some of the supermarket shopping if that's okay with you. One other woman here has a car and she and I rotate doing that."

"I would love to help in any way I can."

"You sure are beautiful. Don't you think so, Roman?"

"You sound like Nina. Why does everyone want to make sure I'm noticing. Yes, she is beautiful and so are you, Aunt Vi."

She chuckled and rolled her eyes at him.

"Charmer," she replied. "Do you have things with you like clothes or other belongings?"

"Yes."

"Roman, go get her things out of her car while she and I talk and take a roll with you before you complain about having to stop eating them. I swear, I don't know how you stay in such good shape with the way you eat, especially rolls."

Roman stood.

"I have to stay in shape in order to keep eating all this good food you cook. I'll get her things," he said as Marissa handed him her car keys. He nodded when she mouthed a word of thanks.

Roman walked out of the kitchen and smiled as he watched his aunt work her charm on Marissa, making sure she felt welcomed. He was glad they were unable to see the extra pep in his step as he left the house.

10

Halloween wasn't one of Roman's favorite holidays. This day gave adults a pass for crazy, wild behavior. Today, he was going to be working a double shift, starting with his late-night shift working well into the next evening. This was one night each year where their captain asked everyone to work overtime knowing the streets would be filled with adults in kids dressed in tame to wild when it came to attire.

Today, he was feeling extra excited and a bit happier than he'd been in a long time. Nina was excited about the harvest fest occurring at their church and he was currently on his way to drop her off and his father would pick her up later. While she had been at school, he'd had a chance to stop at his aunt's place to check in to see how things were going with Marissa.

Over a month had passed since she'd began living at the house and he found himself stopping by several times during those weeks with one excuse after another for his presence when the truth was, he just wanted to see Marissa. One evening, he stayed for dinner and hung around after to help Marissa, who had volunteered to clean up the kitchen. That was one of many occasions that he was able to learn more about her and as much as he tried to fight it, he was drawn to her and not in a way that made her look like a damsel in distress. She was more than that. They talked about desires of the heart when it came to work, friendship and love. He could see that despite where life had taken her over the years, she wanted more – she wanted better. She shared that she couldn't erase her past, but she could learn from it and be a better person, first for herself and then for her daughter. He respected that and could see how passionate she was about finding her perfect niche in life. They agreed that no life is always perfect, but the vision for said life could be perfect as they worked toward it. That's the kind of woman he found himself longing for and dreaming about. He didn't judge her past, but he wanted the kind of woman who looked toward the future and its prosperity.

They even talked about God and church and he shared what his faith meant to him. Marissa was hesitant to share at first, but after he'd put his heart and soul on the line about his love for Christ, she told him about her doubts and how she never trusted the love of God because her life seemed so hard. She then told him that after being angry with herself and God, she knew that he would never put more on her than she could handle and because he birthed in her a strong, black woman, she knew that she'd survive through anything. Meeting him had been a testament that every man in her life wouldn't want something from her that compromised her dignity.

There was a friendship growing between them that neither expected, but they both stood on the outside watching to see where things would go. He wasn't in a rush. He wanted to enjoy getting to know the woman who was a mystery to him over a month ago and now he found himself smiling and thinking about her when they were apart.

Marissa had become more than the woman living in her car that he'd encountered that night. Though when they talked, they stayed away from any conversation that dived too deep into her life. He could see that some parts she wasn't ready to share with him and to make sure she never felt ashamed in his company, he gladly let her lead where their conversations went.

She'd shared that due to the help of his mother and aunt, she had taken several computer classes and was looking forward to going on several job interviews soon. Through job training, without knowing it, she had strong office skills and a killer personality and one-thousand-watt smile that charmed everyone she met. Since she had never had to interview for a job before, though she didn't share why, she wasn't comfortable with how to conduct herself. His aunt was able to help her sign up for a class regarding how to enhance her interview skills. His mother and aunt were already setting up interviews for her and she was excited. Seeing her happy made his day.

On one additional evening when he'd had Nina with him, he'd stayed around to fix a leaking pipe in one of the bathrooms and when he walked into the family room of the house, Nina was sitting comfortably on the brown sectional with Marissa watching the Wizard of Oz, her favorite movie. He didn't dare interrupt them and instead, sat down and joined them. His aunt had made Nina a bowl of popcorn which they enjoyed together. He was drawn to Marissa and even his aunt made a comment about his increased visits and mentioned that she could tell he was smitten with her. He hadn't heard that word in a long time, but it was descriptive of what was happening. He was intrigued by her desire to get out of her situation and find her place in life.

During one of his visits, he brought of the topic of her daughter and her parents again and after some coaxing, he'd convinced her to pay them a visit and try to mend their broken relationship. She hadn't even told them that she was living back in Philadelphia. Times when they would allow her to talk to Lacey, she still didn't let them know that she was working on changing her life. He didn't know what had happened to their relationship, but he prayed that their bond would soon be strengthened and she could spend quality time with the daughter she missed so much.

Whenever he showed up with Nina, Marissa turned gloomy, not at Nina, but over how much she missed her own daughter, something he understood. Each time he visited, he encouraged her to do something about it. He didn't want to push her too hard, but he saw the longing in her eyes.

Now that he knew who Lacey was, he realized she and Nina were friends. He'd heard his daughter mentioned her friends, especially Lacey on several occasions and remembered her once saying Lacey was like her and didn't have a mother. She knew that her mother had died and mentioned that Lacey's mother wasn't dead, she just didn't live with her, but she wanted to. There was no way he was going to allow Marissa to miss out on a chance to have a relationship with her daughter. Everyone deserved a second and even a third chance. Whatever Marissa had done was in her past.

As he and Nina drove toward the church for the harvest festival, his thoughts turned back to the conversation he'd had earlier in the day with Marissa.

He saw so much growth and potential in who she could be and in who she wanted to be. He thought that after helping her get settled into a place where he knew she would receive the support and encouragement she needed to take control of her life, he would go back to his life and not be as consumed with making sure she didn't falter. That hasn't happened and it's been over a month since their first encounter. He was overjoyed at the progress she'd already made.

When he arrived at her house a few hours ago, he thought perhaps Marissa had been out running errands because after parking, he didn't see her car anywhere and it was easy to spot amongst cars not as high-end as hers. Knowing he had some time before he had to leave to, he waited around and checked to see if there was anything his aunt needed him to do. Once inside, the first person he saw was Marissa. She was vacuuming the carpeted living room. Before disturbing her with her back to him, he watched her move about and instantly, the connection he'd felt with her from the moment they'd first met filled the space they were in. What he felt wasn't just physical attraction, though she was stunningly beautiful, but it was a connection on a more personal, heartfelt level. He had tried to give a name to what he felt, but still couldn't find one. His heart smiled like the smile on his face every time he thought about her. When he saw his aunt come around the corner from the kitchen, catching him staring at Marissa, she cleared her throat and the moment was interrupted. Marissa looked her way and followed her gaze to him.

"Roman! You're here. Are you bringing another lovely soul like Marissa?" Vi asked the moment Marissa cut the vacuum machine off.

"No, Nina and I are on our way to the church soon and I wanted to stop by. There's a meeting with Pastor

Battle about the community fair next weekend and she wants to go over the security for that day. I hope you're all planning to come. There will be carnival rides, food, music, games and of course booths will be set up for anyone who needs services provided by the city and the state."

"I love your pastor. Everything she does is for the people," Vi said.

"She is the best," he said and then his eyes landed on Marissa.

"Hello," she said.

"Hi there. Still settling in nicely?" he asked.

"I've more than settled in. Your aunt is a lifesaver, but I'm sure you already knew that."

"How long are you hanging around. You seem to be doing that a lot lately."

Roman could have kicked himself as his aunt laughed knowing that she was being obvious about addressing the elephant in the room which was before Marissa arrived, she'd never seen this much of him in a week.

"Briefly," he said. Though his aunt was addressing him, his eyes were still locked with Marissa's.

"Well, let me at least make you and Nina a sandwich and get you some fruit to take with you to the church."

"Thanks, aunt Vi," he said to her back and she hustled off to the kitchen.

"So, you're headed to church, huh? You spend a lot

of time at church," Marissa said.

"I do. I enjoy it and so does my daughter."

"I loved church when I was a young girl."

"Do you still desire to go to church? I know you mentioned some struggles with church, but every church is not like the one where you had the bad experience," he said.

"I haven't been to church in a lot of years, not since before Lacey was born. I'm not the kind of person people in church want around," she said, softly and shyly while looking down at the floor.

"Don't do that," Roman said immediately and walked closer to her.

"Don't do what?" Marissa asked without lifting her head.

"Look at me."

Roman waited for her head to lift up and for her eyes to meet his. When she did, he spoke from his heart.

"I'm sorry. I don't do well looking people in the eye. I always feel like they can see through me and won't like what they see," she admitted.

Roman had no problem admitting everything he saw and knew about her he liked. He wanted her to see and know her own self-worth.

"I know life has been hard for you. I feel like what you've gone through has made you feel like you're not worthy enough for anything or anyone and that's not true. I know people have an image of what a church person is supposed to be and that they're all judgmental. I can't speak for them all, but not everyone is like that. There is no special type of person who should be in a church. Yes, there are always going to be naysayers just like out in the real world, but God loves everyone and yes, you, too."

"You don't know the things I've done."

"What you've done doesn't matter. There are situations in which people tend to hold over your head your entire life, never forgiving and never letting you forget, but trust me, that's not all people. It's not me. It's not my pastor. It's not my aunt or my family. I wasn't raised that way," Roman explained.

"Your family seems great and I say that after only meeting you and your aunt. Not all families are like that. Mine isn't and neither is the church where I grew up."

"Every church isn't like that. One day, take a leap and visit my church. I can't say everyone is inviting, but in general, the atmosphere is one of welcoming, acceptance and unconditional love. Church also builds you up to deal with those who want to chastise or put you down for the things they think they know about you, but God can give you the strength to deal with those kinds of people, causing them to take another look at themselves before they judge you. My aunt seems quite taken by you."

Marissa smile bright which made Roman's heart burst with joy.

"She is amazing."

"What about your family? Are you still going to reach out to them today? You said you were hoping to see Lacey in her costume."

He knew it was a pained point for her and even though he knew she struggled with her relationship with them, he felt that with time, all things were possible.

"I haven't yet, but I will today. I'm still not sure if I'm ready yet, but I do miss Lacey. I want to be a daily presence in her life if my mom will let me."

"You have rights, Marissa. I know it's been years, but you still have rights and you're trying. That will count for something," he said.

"Not with my mother it won't."

"It's a good thing your mother isn't the only authority over this situation. I know you've struggled with it and I'm going to continue to encourage you and pray for your situation because you may not think so, but Lacey needs you in her life. All little girls need their mothers. I believe even your mother's heart will soften when she sees you are trying. Keep working on that. They love you and I bet that little lady of yours would love to see you."

"I do miss, Lacey. I miss her so much. I think about her every night before I go to sleep and every move I'd like to make in life, I'm trying to make work because I want to be in her life."

"Then do it. I didn't see your car when I pulled up. I

wasn't sure you were here."

"Oh, yeah, I sold it," she said.

"You sold it?"

"I did and I bought something more reasonable. I was able to save a lot of money from the sale since it was paid for. One day, I'll be able to make a move to my own place and have a room for Lacey. A car is a car and I didn't need one that flashy, drawing the wrong attention. This is a nice neighborhood, but really, I was driving a new BMW and I'm pretty much homeless. How crazy is that?" she asked and laughed.

"Well, you're not homeless," he said, laughing with her.

"I know, but you know what I'm saying. I bought a sensible Honda and I even tried to give some of the money from the sale to your aunt for all that's she's done for me and she wouldn't take it. I feel like I should do more."

"I know my aunt and she will never, ever take money from you."

"I get that now which is why I'm now in charge of cleaning duty. It's the least I can do."

"I know she appreciates it. Maybe you'll come with her and the rest of the ladies here at the house to the community fair my church is having next weekend. I think you'll enjoy it," he said.

"I don't know. I may run into someone I know and that may not be good," she said.

"Don't let people keep you from living. I have a

feeling people have been taking from you for a long time."

"You have no idea. I could tell you some things, but then again, it may taint your image of who I am."

"Nothing could ever do that, no matter how bad. As long as you're not currently breaking the law, I'm good and I don't judge. It's not my place even as a police officer. Perhaps you could use an honest ear and if so, I can be that ear, if you'd like. Maybe over coffee one day or dinner one evening?" he asked.

There. He'd said it and shocked himself. The words came out before he could think of what he was saying and offering. Never had he ever asked someone out that he'd pulled over or come upon on the other end of his profession, but he already struggled with the fact that there was something about Marissa that he couldn't shake. He wasn't sure she was up to it or even interested. She was trying to get herself together and probably not interested in coffee or dinner with anyone, even him.

He could see the wheels turning in her head at the idea he just put in the atmosphere. She was probably wondering if he had actually asked her out or if he was still just being nice because she was down on her luck.

The air thickened between them and he saw her about to speak when his aunt entered the room again.

"Here's something for you and Nina to snack on while you drive to the church," she said.

"Thank you," he said.

"What's going on here?" she asked looking between them. "Looks like I'm interrupting a moment," she said.

Feeling like he'd put Marissa in a terrible predicament of trying to decipher the meaning behind his request for dinner, he figured he'd let her off the hook by leaving. Perhaps after what she'd been through, she didn't want to think about going on a date with anyone.

"No, nothing at all. I was just leaving," he said and called out for Nina who raced by him out the door and to the car. He berated himself as he walked down the steps of the house and rushed to his car.

"Yes!"

Roman stopped in his tracks and turned around. Standing on the top step after following him out was Marissa. She looked nervous, but he was sure he'd heard her say yes.

"Yes?" he asked.

She smiled at him and his heart sped up rapidly.

"Yes, to coffee or dinner," she said.

"How about coffee and dinner?" he asked.

"Okay, coffee and dinner. Are you sure?" she asked.

"No, but it feels right."

"Does it? Is it because you feel like you need to take care of me because I'm down on my luck? I've heard about that," she said.

"Not at all. I have a feeling you can take care of yourself and you don't need anyone in your space out of curiosity or need. I don't see you in need of male companionship of any kind, not even a date. I may have that first day, but I'm beyond that and so are you. Dinner between two new friends?" he asked.

"Yes. Dinner between two new friends."

"Well, it's Friday and I'm working tonight and tomorrow, but how about Sunday evening. I can pick you up or you can meet me, whichever makes you more comfortable."

"How about you tell me where and I'll meet you there," she offered.

Roman thought of his favorite restaurant.

"Do you like Italian food?" he asked.

"I love Italian food."

Roman gave her the name of his favorite Italian restaurant and gave her the address when she took her phone out of her back pocket and keyed the information in.

"Five o'clock Sunday? I'll make a reservation," he said.

"I'll see you there."

Roman didn't want to say anything else and ruin ending their conversation on a high note. He waved and got in his car. He smiled when he saw her wave back as he pulled away from the curb.

"What was that?" he said out loud.

"Huh?" Nina exclaimed from the backseat.

"Oh, nothing. Daddy was thinking out loud."

In his head, he heard the soft voice of his wife tell

him, "you already know."

Now at the church after chowing down on the roast beef sandwich his aunt had fixed him, he walked toward the pastor's office after dropping Nina off in the fellowship hall. He'd planned a meeting knowing he would be at the church. He hoped he'd be able to take his mind off of Marissa long enough to focus. He was more than excited over their upcoming date. This time, it wasn't a set up by one of his friends. He'd met a woman that he'd never thought he'd be attracted to, but here he was, looking forward to seeing her again soon.

11

Marissa checked herself in the rear-view mirror of her car, not sure what she was trying to fix. Her parents knew her and she needed to be herself. After Roman had left to go to his church, she changed and nervously called her parents. After explaining to them she was in town and hoped to see Lacey in her costume, they agreed to allow her to come over. She was halfway out of the door while she talked to them. Her father mentioned they were going to an event at their church, but if she came by soon, she would have some time with Lacey before they left. She drove fast, but safe to their house.

She parked and walked on shaky legs to their house. She was glad that a few days ago, in order to be prepared for any job interviews, she'd purchased a brand new black and white pants suit and instead of the usual high heels she often wore, she had purchased a sensible pair of black flats. Her natural hair was blown out straight and she wore it down, flowing around her shoulders and unusual for her, she wore very light makeup. She was about to ring the bell when the inside door swung open and on the other side stood her mother, stoned face and again, as usual, emotionless.

"Marissa," Martika said greeting her daughter. "This is a new look for you."

"Stop it, Mar," William said from behind her. "The girl has been here for one second and you're already out for the kill. Give it a rest. She's here for Lacey, not to fight with you. Come on in, Marissa," he added.

"Mom, dad," Marissa said greeting them with a slight wave. She dared not go in for a hug knowing her mother's response would be to stiffen.

"You look nice," he said.

"Thanks, daddy. I just bought this."

"Come in and have a seat. Lacey is a few doors down the street at a friend's house comparing outfits. How was your drive into Philly?" he asked.

Marissa looked from her father to her mother who now sat on the sofa across from her. She quickly looked around the room and was surprised to see pictures of herself staring back at her from years ago. She was sure her mother had destroyed them all. She then locked eyes with them again.

"Actually, I'm no longer living in Jersey. When I told you over the phone that I was here, what I didn't say was that I now live here in Philly. I've been back for almost two months," she explained.

"You what? Since when? You didn't tell us in the times you've called and even talked face to face with

Lacey on the phone. Why didn't you tell us?" her mother asked, with a cold, piercing tone to her words.

"I didn't think it mattered to you. Things haven't been the best and I was trying to focus on getting my life in order."

"You're working on you – that's good to know," William said.

"Are you back alone or did you bring that man with you?" her mother asked.

"Martika, pull it back, sweetheart. This is not an inquisition. We talked about this," William said as he smiled at Marissa.

"It's okay, daddy. No, I'm here alone. I left that life in Jersey. I'm staying at a transitional house while I figure out what I'm going to do with my life. I've been taking some computer classes, some classes to improve my interview skills and looking over information to possibly take some college classes."

"Wow! That's amazing! I'm happy for you," William said.

"Transitional house? What is that? You're living in some house with a bunch of strangers?" her mother asked.

"It's run by a nice woman and her sister. They have several houses across the city. This one has other women and a few children and they help with services to help women get back up on their feet after falling off."

"Is that what you did? You fell off?" her mother

asked.

"Martika!" William chided.

Marissa watched their exchanged.

"I simply asked a question. We're having a conversation, right? I'm conversing," Martika said and turned back to Marissa.

"I've made some bad choices and my decisions haven't been the best, but I'm trying."

"Tired of what you were doing?" she asked.

"Tired of a lot of things, but it's more about being a better person for my daughter. I want to be able to see more of Lacey."

"She will love that," William said.

"We'll see about that. I haven't said yes to anything other than you seeing her today. I don't want her routine disturbed by your impromptu visits."

"She's her mother, Martika. Stop it. I think it's great that you're trying and Lacey will be excited about more time with you. Every time she talks to you, she spends days waiting to talk to you again. She really loves when she can see you face to face on the phone and when she sees that you're here, she'll be over the moon with excitement."

"Why don't you go get Lacey and Marissa and I can talk," Martika said.

"No way. I'll get back and Marissa will be gone if I know you. I'll sit here with her and you go get Lacey," he said.

Martika didn't comment, but sucked her teeth as

she stood and stomped off toward the front door. As soon as the door closed behind her, Marissa exhaled.

"Thanks, daddy."

"I know it doesn't seem like it, but your mother will eventually get over her anger. I tried talking to her and it's going to take some time."

"Mom and I both are to blame for what has become of our relationship and I understand her anger, though I'm surprised she's still mad. I hope she doesn't let Lacey see her being this angry over me."

"Never. I would never allow that and she knows it. She's never said one bad word about you to Lacey and she never would. She loves that baby too much to speak ill of you. Despite your absence, Lacey loves you so much. She runs around here saying mommy this and mommy that and when you send her stuff, especially that pink rhino, she never lets that stuff go. That rhino is her favorite toy and she sleeps with it every night. She has pictures of you in her room from the ones you've sent on my phone. I downloaded a few and printed them out for her. She insisted I put them in a frame. So, I don't want you to feel awkward or out of place in your daughter's life. It's time you repaired the damage done by your absence and start with Lacey. Your mother and I will be fine. Your mother, as you can see is a work in progress. I'm glad you're back," William said.

Marissa looked at him and tears fell from her eyes. For the first time in years, she heard her father's voice crack. He was near tears himself.

"I'm sorry, daddy. I'm so sorry for everything I've done. I didn't mean to hurt you and mommy. I was being selfish and only thought of myself. I'll never disappear again and I hope you and mommy can forgive me."

William reached out his hands to her and she placed her small ones into his larger ones as he gripped them tight.

"Rissa, everyone makes mistakes and who am I to judge. God is the only judge and jury and he is a forgiving God. Why would I not be? All of that is in the past and it's the present and future that we all have to work on. If there is anything I can do to help you find your way, you know where to find me."

"Thank you, daddy. Maybe one day, if you don't find it robbery of your time, we can go for coffee or something. I don't mean to leave mom out, but I don't think she'd come."

William chuckled.

"I agree. Baby steps with her."

Before the conversation could continue, the front door opened and Marissa saw a flash of pink come barreling through the door. When her eyes landed on Lacey, her heart was about to bust with joy over being able to see her in person.

"Lacey, look who's here," William said.

Lacey, who had been working to get her coat off had yet to look her way. When she did, her eyes lit up and she ran so fast toward her, Marissa barely had time to prepare for the leap Lacey took into her arms. She had seconds to open her arms to grab her up.

"Mommy!" Lacey screamed and hugged her so tight around the neck, Marissa had to take small breaths to breathe. She didn't care. Her baby was in her arms.

"Oh, my goodness. You've gotten so big. You look even bigger than you do on the phone and you're beautiful."

"I miss you, mommy."

"I miss you, too. You look pretty in this pink dress."

"I'm Cinderella. We're going to church. Are you coming with us?" Lacey asked.

Marissa looked at her parents and then back to Lacey who was now back on the floor on her feet.

"Well, not this time, but maybe soon. I came to spend a little time with you before you went to church."

"Only for a little while? Are you going to come back again?" Lacey asked.

"Yes, she will. Why don't you show your mommy your room? She hasn't seen your new furniture. You can also show her all the toys and things that she's sent you that you still have."

"Yea! I can show you all of the toys and dolls I have."

Marissa smiled as Lacey jumped up and down, clapping happily. She wanted to cry at the happy moment realizing how many days and nights of seeing her own daughter this happy that she's missed out on. Before she could think too hard on it, Lacey pulled her by the hand toward the stairs. She said a quiet thanks to whatever force surrounded her and was responsible for making this visit possible.

**

"Thanks for the extra security you're putting in place for the community fair. I want to go all out for this and our top priority is the safety of everyone in attendance," Pastor Battle said to the men and women who were gathered in her office at the church. While the harvest festival took place in another part of the church, they were getting a chance to talk about the church and community fair that was coming up.

"We have everything under control along with a few officers from the force who are off that day and are happy to volunteer their time," Roman said.

"Great. I think we're done here unless there's anything else?" she asked looking around locking eyes with everyone.

"Nothing I can think of," Roman said as everyone filed out of the office. Then one last thing came to mind. There is one thing about that weekend. I have a note on my calendar that Deacon Battle is flying back into town that morning. Do you need me to send someone to pick him up at the airport?" he added.

Roman wasn't assigned to security for the pastor's husband that weekend, but he always checked to be sure business around them was taken care of.

"That would be great. I was going to pick him up, but my kids will go crazy knowing the setup for the fair would be going on while we wait at the airport for their father," she said.

"Don't worry about it. I don't have the specifics on his flight, but I can check with him on it," Roman said.

"I have it if you can wait around for a few minutes. I can pull it up for you. "

"Okay, that works. I can get someone on that by tomorrow morning," he said.

Roman sat back down and logged back into his iPad to open up his schedule. Surprisingly, the first thing that popped up was a reminder about his dinner date with Marissa. Just seeing her name made him smile.

"You're smiling mighty bright," Pastor Battle said catching Roman off guard.

He tried to hide his delight at seeing Marissa name, but it was too late.

"Am I? I didn't realize it."

"I know that smile. It's the one I see on my husband's face right before he tells me he can't wait until we have some down time together. I know that look and something tells me it's a woman," she said.

Roman shook his head, but didn't deny her assumption.

"To be honest, I think I'm in over my head."

"Over a woman? I don't believe that. I know you and you have the spirit of discernment. You know what's good for you and what's not."

"Yes, it's a woman and it's a weird situation, but I think I really like her and I hardly know her. What I do know is that she wouldn't be a woman I would usually think about bonding or connecting with based on how we met."

"You can meet the woman of your dreams anywhere. God is funny like that. I don't tell many people this, but when I met my husband, he was selling bootleg music and movies out of his car. He was with some other men and he approached me. I questioned him about his profession of choice and he said he was only trying to make ends meet while in college. I didn't judge him, but I did make it clear that if he was interested in me, he needed a legitimate job, nothing that was taking money from someone else's hard work. He asked for my number and I told him if he was meant to meet me again at a time when he was on the up and up, he would. A few weeks later, I went to a diner with some friends from college that was so far out of the way, there wasn't much transportation that carried you there. When we sat down, guess who was our waiter?"

"Deacon Battle?" Roman asked and laughed.

"Sure was. He couldn't wait to tell me how I changed him that night because he told his friends he'd just met the woman he was going to marry one day and he had to be a person I would want. He gave up that illegal activity and found a job. He had a clunker of a car, but it got him from campus to that diner. We try to go to that place once a year and we laugh and talk about how that night was the start of the rest of our lives together. I was a preacher's kid and there was no way I was going to get hooked up with someone doing anything illegal. He made the choice to turn his life around and when the time was right, God sent me to that diner on the night that he was working. I mean it was far out. God has a sense of humor and when you think you have your life all planned out and you know what your next move will be, He steps in and shows you that He is always in control and He knows what's best for you. Don't question yourself when it comes to this young lady. If you feel like she's someone you want to find a place in your heart for, don't run from it. Embrace it and let God show you that He can give you the desires of your heart and I know you've struggled over dating or not dating and wanting someone who is ready for something serious and not something casual. Sounds like you're investing effort in this woman and if so, I'm happy for you. It's time," she said.

Roman shook his head, acknowledging her opinion and as usual, he appreciated her honesty.

"Whew, you hit that on the head," he replied.

"You know I've been pulling for you. You're a man serious about his faith, his family and definitely about his heart. I knew the moment the right woman, no matter who she is who where she came from, entered your life, you wouldn't miss that blessing. Is it someone here at the church?"

"No. Remember I told you about the young lady I came across one night while working? The one that had been sleeping in her car?"

"I do remember you telling me about that. I hope things worked out well for her."

"She's staying at my aunt's place and she's doing okay. I asked her out for dinner," he said. Roman waited for some kind of reaction, but didn't get any. Perhaps she would tell him that he should proceed cautiously.

"I hope you're taking her someplace nice," she said. Roman smiled.

"That's it? You're not going to say more?"

"What more were you expecting? Each time I've seen you and you've mentioned this young woman, you smile like you've won the lottery even though until today, you didn't mention your interest in her on a personal level. Whoever she is, I already know she's pretty special to you. It's been a long time since I've seen you smile like that. Go with it and allow yourself to enjoy her company. I can tell you really want to."

"She's different. She has a past where a lot of it's a mystery and whatever it is, it's caused a strain with her family. I shouldn't be attracted to her considering how I met her."

"You told me that story and all I can say is we all have a past. No sin is bigger than the other – it's all sin. I know people say that your past dictates your future, but it doesn't have to if you don't want it to. Whatever her past is, it hasn't stopped you from being interested in her and it shouldn't. Have you ever thought that you crossing paths with her was God's interference in both of your lives, knowing what each of you needed most? Without knowing her story, I would say she probably needed someone who reached out to her with a helping hand without judgement and I know you, Roman, that's exactly what you did. In you, you needed to see that you are making a difference, not just in her life, but in everything that you do. Not only did God show that to you, but he showed you how to have compassion for a woman who He brought into your life for a purpose. Any other officer could have gotten that call that night, but it was you. God has a way of bringing things together, making wrongs, right and opening eyes to the possibilities. Go with what your heart is telling you and don't worry about who she was. Instead, focus on who she is right now. Clearly, she's someone special if she's drawn your interest. I hope you're going to invite her to church soon. I look forward to meeting her. This woman has brought a genuine smile back to your face, so yeah, I would love to meet her."

Roman smiled.

"You know I'm always inviting people to church and I mentioned it to her, especially the community fair that's coming up. I'm hoping she'll come to that.

She's had some church-hurt in the past, so I don't want to push her."

"I understand that and I agree. When she's ready, she will come to this church or perhaps another church. Any woman who meets you and has any interest in you will know how important church and God is to your life and she won't be able to stay away from those things the fuel you."

"Thank you, Pastor. I'll let you get out to the harvest festival. I'm going to hang around a little longer with Nina and then I'll leave her here for my dad to pick her up and take her home with him."

"Good luck Sunday evening," she said.

"From your mouth to God's ears," he said.

12

Roman arrived at the restaurant thirty minutes early just in case Marissa showed up early. He didn't want her left alone waiting for him. Waiting for her in the lobby of the restaurant to avoid standing outside in the chilly November weather, his patience with himself and his nervousness annoyed not just him, but most likely the staff as well who offered to sit him early while he waited on Marissa. He felt like a teenage boy out on his first date and hoping the girl he was waiting to arrive would like him. He was thankful they would be seated at a table where he could see the door. He'd sent her a text to let him know when she arrived so that he could meet her at her car. Thinking she would text or call him any minute, he was surprised to look up and see her talking to the hostess in the lobby. He stood as she approached.

"Hello," he said when she reached the table. He walked around to help her out of her coat.

"Hi. I hope you weren't waiting too long," Marissa said.

"I was waiting for you to text when you arrived so

that I could meet you at your car. This is Philly. The streets aren't as safe as I'd like them to be."

"I know. I forgot and by the time I remembered, I was already at the restaurant door. I'm sorry about that."

"No problem. I'm glad you made it. You look beautiful."

Marissa smiled as she took her seat. She'd been so indecisive for the past two days about what to wear after spending an entire day shopping for the perfect outfit. She hoped the purple dress would be okay. It was her favorite color.

"Thank you."

Roman took his seat after she sat down and realized he couldn't stop looking at her. When she caught him staring, he looked away.

"I'm sorry about that. I didn't mean to stare. I'm admiring your beauty and your hair is different."

"You noticed that? I don't wear my own hair down often. I have been wearing wigs for so long, I forgot I had long, healthy hear underneath. You look nice too. You look all GQ-ish in your all black sweater and pants."

"I appreciate that you noticed. Did you have any problems finding the place?" he asked.

"Your directions were perfect. I didn't even have to use the GPS. This place looks nice."

"It's the perfect spot if you like Italian food."

"I love Italian. It's my favorite, though I do have a

penchant for cheesesteaks. I'm a homegrown, Philly girl at heart!" she laughed.

"We'll have to do that sometime. I have a favorite spot I'd love to take you to," Roman said.

"I'd like that. What do you enjoy most here?" she asked, picking up the menu."

"I have many, but if I had to choose one, it would be the Shrimp Carbonaro in this wine sauce that is to die for. I'm thinking of getting it tonight."

"I've been thinking about lasagna all day."

"I've had that and it's fantastic."

Roman looked up and walking in his direction was Dave, a friend and officer from the force. He stood as Dave and his wife, Monica came up to their table.

"Roman! Fancy seeing you here," Dave said greeting him with a handshake. "You remember my wife, Monica," he said.

"I do. Nice seeing you again, Monica."

Roman turned to Marissa when Dave and Monica's attention turned to her, too.

"Good to see you, Roman," Monica said.

"This is Marissa," Roman said introducing her.

"Hello," Marissa said softly as she hurriedly looked in their direction and then back down at the table. She remembered Dave and wondered if he remembered her.

Roman was about to speak when Dave looked at him and then over to Marissa.

"You look familiar. I think we've met before," Dave

said looking from Marissa and then over at Roman, questionably.

Roman tried to change the subject the minute he saw the look of familiarity on Marissa's face. He knew she remembered meeting Dave.

"Out for a date night?" Roman asked, hoping to shift the attention back to Dave and way from Marissa who looked like any minute she was about to bolt from the table.

"Yeah, we are. I remember where I saw you before. Parked in a car during a call Roman and I took. It's odd seeing the two of you here together. Honey, why don't you go ahead and call and check on the kids before we head to the movies while I chat with Roman a bit. Marissa, you don't mind if I borrow Roman for a minute, do you?" he asked without waiting for a response before nudging Roman to stand.

Walking ahead, Dave turned and walked toward the lobby with Roman in tow.

"Make it quick, Dave," Roman said when they reached a corner of the lobby where no other patrons were standing. Dave spotted his wife off to the side on her cell phone talking to their babysitter for the evening.

"Don't try that, make it quick, Dave to me. What are you doing with that woman? Are you out on a date? I remember her. She's the woman who had been sleeping in her car."

"Yes, it is. So what?" Roman asked.

"So, what? So, what is the fact that she was sleeping and probably living in her car and now you're out with her? What's going on?" Dave asked.

"Nothing's going on. We're having dinner, that's all."

"Dude, are you desperate for a date?" Dave joked.

"Not funny, man. Don't disrespect her like that."

"Dude, you're talking about me disrespecting a woman found living in her car. Anyone sleeping in a car like that can afford a place to live. What are you thinking being out with her? How did you connect with her anyway?" Dave asked.

"I'm out with her because I want to be and how I connected with her is not a topic for discussion."

"Man, I'm just looking out for you. Do you even know what she was into? Where she came from? Where the car came from and why she was sleeping in it on a Philly street? Drugs? Gang? Prostitute, maybe?" Dave asked.

Roman's patience had officially worn off.

"Stop trying to be judge and jury. Whatever was or is going on in her life is none of your business or mine."

"Wait, you're out with her and you didn't ask those questions? You're a cop, man. She could have been into something illegal. She's pretty and all, but what do you know about her?" Dave asked.

"We're cool and all, but don't question my personal life. I don't question yours," Roman said feeling himself getting angry and territorial when it came to Marissa.

Dave took a step back as soon as he heard the words, knowing the meaning behind them. He looked in Monica's direction, happy that she was still on the phone.

"Hey, you know that in confidence and I'm not all out in the open in restaurants with mine," Dave said.

"That's not what this is with Marissa. She's not a chick on the side as is your situation and I don't judge you. I don't like it, but your marriage is your business and what you do outside of it is none of my business and it doesn't matter how much of it you like to share. I'm out with Marissa because I want to be and unlike you, I'm not concerned about any part of her life that she hasn't or doesn't want to share with me. I asked her out for dinner and we're having a great time. Looks like Monica is off the phone. You may not want her to hear this conversation. I'll catch you at the station."

"Hey, I didn't mean to cause any tension between us," Dave said.

"Glass houses, Dave. Glass houses. We're good. I'll see you next shift. I'm on later tonight. You?" Roman asked.

"Yeah, I am. Monica and I are heading to a movie and then I'm going to grab some quick shut eye and then I'll see you at the station," Dave said as Monica walked up and joined her arm with his.

"Good to see you out and enjoying yourself on a date. I told Dave when we first spotted you that I haven't seen you smile that hard or laugh in a long time. It's good to see you doing well."

Roman smiled knowing Monica was making reference to Melanie's death and the stupor he'd been in ever since. He'd tried everything, even counseling to shake off the guilt he felt over not being able to do anything to save her, but life had to move forward and he was trying to do that. Tonight, was a good start.

"Thank you and I hope to see the two of you soon. The church is having the community fair soon and we could use a lot of help if you're free?" Roman asked her.

"If it's a Saturday, I'm free. I'll call the church to see what I can do to help."

"I appreciate it and Dave, we could use some extra help with security."

"Anything you need. We can chat about it tonight. We'll let you get back to your date."

Roman nodded and turned back to Marissa.

When he arrived at the table, she was grabbing her coat from the spare chair as if she was preparing to leave.

"I'll leave my share of the cost of dinner. I had a great time," Marissa said trying to slide her coat on without standing.

Roman was stunned and didn't know what happened.

"You're leaving? Why? What's wrong?" he asked.

Marissa stopped moving and looked over at him.

"Are you going to say something like you have an emergency or something and you have to leave? I saw how your friend looked at me. He had that same look of disgust I've seen one too many times. Now, you're embarrassed that one of your friends saw us, right? It's okay, I'm not foreign to that kind of treatment."

Roman sat stunned at the sudden turn of events as Marissa stood. He stood with her.

"Why are you leaving? I'm not going anywhere and I'm not about to come up with some excuse to shorten our dinner. What happened?"

"Your friend happened. He remembered me from that night in my car. I remember him too and I'm sure he told you to run for the hills."

"Marissa, please sit down. I'm not Dave. Did you see any untoward or looks of disgust on my face any this evening, even when they showed up? This isn't about them. I am enjoying your company and I really thought you were enjoying mine," he said.

"I was. I mean I am."

"Then why are you leaving and tossing money on the table? I asked you out tonight. The dinner is on me and I was hoping you didn't have to rush off. If you really want to leave, I'll be okay with it, but I don't understand."

"Really? You want to stay?" she asked quietly. "I feel like everyone is looking at me now."

"Well, they may be considering we're standing here holding a conversation in the middle of the restaurant. Please stay unless you're really uncomfortable and want to leave."

"I don't want to leave. I thought you were going to say you had to leave and I was trying to beat you to the punch."

Roman sat back down and hoped Marissa would, too. He exhaled a sigh of relief when she placed her coat back over the extra chair and sat back down, grabbing the money she'd placed on the table and putting it back in her bag.

"There is no punch to beat me to. I really am having a great time talking to you tonight."

"I bet your friend had some not so nice things to say about me, didn't he? You can tell me because I'm used to that," she said.

"He asked me what I was doing with you since he remembered where he knew you from. I told him it was none of his business because it's not. Dave is Dave and I am me. I asked you to dinner because I wanted to see you again."

"Why?" she asked catching him off guard.

"Why what?"

"Why did you want to see me again? Doesn't the unknown scare you? You don't know everything about me other than I have parents I don't have the best relationship with, I have a six-year-old daughter who barely knows me, I showed up driving an expensive car with no place to live and if it wasn't for you and your aunt, I'd be out on the street."

"What I do or don't know about you is up to you. If you want to talk about it, I'm here to listen and not judge. I like you and I'm not tossing you out because some guy saw us together and may have issues with it. I don't care and neither should you. I'd like to know more about you and I'd like to share more about me with you."

"I'd like that. You're different. I've never met a guy like you who cares so deeply. I see how you are around your aunt and how willing you are to help out around there and of course, how you've helped me. People don't want to help anyone anymore. This is a world all about self."

"I've never been a selfish kind of person. I'm a man of faith and I believe that no one is perfect, we all have our secrets and things about our lives that are unsavory, but that doesn't make us bad people or people who should be criticized. I can't explain to you why I'm interested in you other than to say I get a nice vibe from you and I'm comfortable around you. I think you're beautiful and I want to know more. Is that okay with you?" he asked.

"Yes. Yes, it is. How about I tell you the quick and dirty version of my story and if you're still interested, I may consider you a saint," she said smiling and laughing out loud.

"Deal!" he said and got comfortable and listened as

she talked.

13

Roman couldn't sleep. Usually when he got off from his shift, he was dead tired. His sister had taken Nina to school giving him plenty of time to himself sleep. He was going to have a court day for a few of his cases, but the judge had an emergency and the cases were postponed to later in the week.

After his dinner with Marissa the night before where they'd stayed until the restaurant closed at ten, he barely got any sleep before his shift began, but he had been enjoying her company and didn't want the night to end. He was still marinating on the things about herself that she'd shared. He knew it was hard for her to share deep, personal parts of her life with him, not knowing if his knack for not judging was only temporary or not, but it wasn't. She had guilt that ran deep over all the things she'd done and how her life had turned out as a result of all the wrong turns she'd taken. He tried to encourage her to let her know that any day above ground is another day to make a change and turn a wrong into a right. He learned a lot about how she ended up in Philly sleeping in her car after leaving her life as Delilah behind. He applauded her for making the step toward getting her life back on a path where she was in total control. The issue with her parents was another thing. Hearing her tell the story of the rocky relationship she's had with her mother for many years bothered him. The discord between them was eating away at her and she couldn't figure out a way for her mother to not see her as Delilah, but to see her as Marissa once again. When she told him about how hard she'd been trying to do things right now, he could hear the heartache in every word.

Thanksgiving was coming up in a few weeks and though Marissa's father had suggested she join them for dinner, she wasn't sure her mother wanted her there. Her mother's quietness did not mean acceptance and she wanted that more than anything. She told him about how she was able to spend about an hour with Lacey before they had to leave to get to a church harvest festival on Halloween. She said her mother barely said a word that wasn't full of criticism and she could sense her keeping a watchful ear and eye as she played with Lacey in her bedroom, ready to pounce at any word that she may say wrong to her own daughter. He wished there was a way to help her heal the brokenness with her mother, but he knew it would take time.

After dinner, he'd walked her to her car and asked that she text him when she got in from their dinner date. He reminded her again that he'd had a great time and he had. He hadn't enjoyed a woman's company in a long time as much as he enjoyed Marissa's. He didn't want to approach her the wrong way or take a liberty that she wasn't going to enjoy, so he asked her if he would be out of place if he gave her a kiss. He didn't want to overstep. Instead of responding with words, Marissa moved closer to him and when she rose up to meet him, he lowered his head and planted a soft kiss on her lips. That was enough because as far as he was concerned, they had plenty of time for longer kisses. Tonight, he wanted to leave her with the feeling that what he was feeling for her was real, not passing, not fleeting and not a step toward getting anything from her other than friendship that he hoped to continue to build on.

When they pulled apart, he saw a look of content, the same feeling he felt. They were on the same page and that quick kiss said so.

"Was that okay?" she had asked, causing his heart to stir. Her tone was loving and unapologetic, yet questionable because even though what was happening between them was still fresh and new, it was obvious they were growing together and she wanted him to see that he wasn't in this thing alone. When he confirmed the kiss was okay along with the fact that she'd taken over the act, he was overwhelmed. Everything about Marissa screamed out to him that she was rescuing his heart and already, he was all in.

He looked into her eyes and held her stare. In his eyes, he wanted her to see his heart because he was wearing it in plain sight for her to see. He wanted her to see a judgement-free zone and a place where anything she told him would remain with him. They may have met in a strange way, but he knew it was meant to be. He wasn't questioning it, but going ahead with being open and showing Marissa that he was a man who was in her corner all the way. She may have gone through a lot, but he could see her heart and it was pure. She was caring and loved deeply, even with a deep love and respect for her mother.

Their dinner date ended without any plans for getting together again and there was no doubt in his mind, he wanted to do that. Grabbing his cell phone, he dialed her number and she answered on the first ring.

"Hi, Roman."

"Hi yourself. I hope you slept well," he said.

"You should be asleep. I see the time and you worked all night after getting no sleep between the end of dinner and the start of your shift. You must be tired," she said.

"I am, but I was thinking about you and I wanted to tell you again how much I enjoyed dinner and was wondering if you'd like to take in a move with me this week. I don't know how busy your schedule is, but I'm even open to a daytime movie if that's better for you," he said hopeful.

"A movie? Sure, that sounds nice. I have a busy day today and tomorrow, but I'm free Wednesday, Thursday and Friday. I know you have your community thing at your church on Saturday," she said.

"I have bible study on Wednesday, but Thursday or Friday works for me. If you ever want to visit my church, it's still an open invitation. I'm not trying to drop that on you, but I want you to know you're always welcome. Let's do a movie on Thursday and this time, I hope you'll let me pick you up instead of meeting me."

"Thursday works and I'll be here when you're ready to pick me up. So, my story last night didn't scare you off?" Marissa asked.

"Why? Did you think I wouldn't call you?" he asked.

"I didn't know."

"Marissa, I meant it when I said I wanted to get to know you and thank you for sharing your story."

"You've done so much for me. I've never had anyone who didn't want something from me that took everything in me to give to them. You're a genuine person and that's rare. Most want something in return for their niceness," she said.

"I don't and I never will. I won't be another man in your life taking advantage of you. I like you and I'm looking forward to a movie and popcorn with extra butter and a gigantic soda," he laughed.

"Me, too."

"Well, maybe if you enjoy the movie, you'll agree to accompany me to the community fair on Saturday. My aunt told me she's going to set up a table to sell those delicious rolls of hers. It's going to be fun. There are huge gigantic tents that will be heated against the cold weather and lots of activities and community services available. We're having lots of food, games and music. If you want, maybe you can bring Lacey if your parents are okay with that. Nina will be there and before you and I ever knew each other, they were friends," he said.

"I know. I asked Lacey about her and she said, and I quote, "we've been friends for years, mommy.""

Roman laughed.

"She said years?" he quipped.

"Can you believe that? These young girls with old souls. I'll ask my parents to see if they want to bring her or if they're okay with me bringing her. I'm not sure about the latter. I called this morning to ask if I could stop by after Lacey got out of school today and my mother quickly brushed it off with some story about them being busy."

"Don't stop trying," he said.

"I know. She makes it hard, but I won't. She did say she'd let Lacey call me before bed tonight, so I'm excited about that. It's something."

"So, movie and community fair?" he asked.

"Can I let you know when we go to the movies?" she asked.

"Absolutely and don't forget what I said about the open invitation to visit my church."

"Do you invite a lot of people to church?" she asked.

"If you're asking if I invite women to church, the answer is yes, but not the way you're thinking. Like you, I shared my life with you last night when we talked and you know about my wife. Her loss has been a struggle for me and since then, I haven't really dated and I haven't invited anyone to church that I may have been dating or anything. I haven't been dating. I often invite people I know to church, men and women, but this isn't some kind of harem thing. I don't have a plethora of women in line with invites to come to church like it's a date. Church is for anyone and I think you'd enjoy the church and my pastor. She's a woman and a very powerful one at that. She's a pastor with a heart as big as this world. She's all about the people."

"I don't know if I'm church material. The things I've done," she said, not completing her statement.

"God is much more forgiving than people," he said.

"Your God doesn't want someone like me in church. I let a man use and abuse me mentally, emotionally and physically because I wanted him and the lifestyle he provided. I didn't even realize that he had no feelings for me; no real feelings at least. How could he if he had no problem with me stripping for money. I was no different to him than the other women he had out on the street making money for him. The only difference was I was also eye candy for him when he needed me to be. I can't imagine any God wanting someone like me in His church."

"Marissa, a church is a place of healing if you need it. I can't promise there won't be judgmental people in the church because a church is comprised of the same element of people you meet out here in the streets. Don't let that deter you. Think about it. There's no pressure. I wouldn't be me if I didn't invite you. I better get some sleep. I'll call or text you about the time for the movie. Looking forward to hanging out again," he said.

"Me, too."

Roman hung up and chuckled.

"You got jokes, huh God? Nowhere in my life would I have suspected you'd let a woman like Marissa walk into my life. She's as broken and torn as I am and yet, we smile and beam like two high school kids when we see and talk to each other. I like her, but you already know that. So, you found a woman the complete opposite of who I would typically connect with and you're building a connection so strong that I can't walk away even if I wanted to, though I don't. I'm smiling again. Yeah, you got jokes, God and you are playing this well," he said before walking into the shower.

14

Marissa walked into the entrance of the community fair and looked around for Roman. She'd sat in her car for almost an hour working up the nerve to go in. At the movies, she promised him she would come for a little while. She was still feeling down that she and her mother couldn't see eye to eye on allowing Lacey to come. Not to be deterred from at least enjoying herself, she told Roman she would meet him at the fair.

Arriving around the time that setup was still going on, Marissa sat nervously in her car, not sure about being around this crowd of people. She hadn't been to church or a church function in years. Still, she could tell everyone showing up had an air of excitement about them, soothing her uneasiness a little. She smiled when Roman drove up earlier and even brighter when she texted to let him know she was on her way, though she was already there.

She watched him work as they prepared for people to arrive. He was right that the fair was going to be a big event. There were stages being set up for entertainment, fun activities for the kids and lots of food vendors. She had offered to bring his Aunt Vi knowing she was going to be selling her rolls, but another person at the house who also had a car and was helping her out for the day was going to bring her to the event.

There were kids running around with excitement for the festivities to begin and her dreams of spending the day with Lacey who she knew would have a good time dashed again when she thought of her mother's rejection. If it wasn't for Roman's friendship and support, she shuddered to think of where she would be right now. As with the past month, she'd ignored every text and phone call from Wayne, demanding that she come back, including the one she received as she was driving to the fair. His last warning gave her comfort that perhaps, he was finally realizing that she wasn't going back. He told her that was his last call and if she never wanted to be anything, then he didn't care either. Little did he know that she was more than he ever appreciated her for. Maybe if she hadn't met Roman, a man who was showing her how a woman should be treat with care and respect, she may have thought that the only kind of man for her would be someone like Wayne. She now knew better and was doing better for herself.

Turning her thoughts away from her old life, she turned them to her date night out to the movies with Roman. Not only did they have a great time taking in an early movie while Nina was in school, they sat down and chatted over ice cream until he had to pick her up from school. They went to one of his favorite burger spots and she felt like a young girl, dating for the first time. They sat on the same side in the booth and at one point, were holding hands under the table as they talked and enjoyed the moment. She had no idea dating could be so fulfilling – something she'd never experienced before. She'd woke that morning with an excitement that had never greeted her before. She went through the clothes she had and took over an hour to pick out the perfect outfit. She applied her makeup carefully and sat nervously in front of the television waiting for Roman to arrive. When she opened the door to his smiling face, her heart was overwhelmed in delight over seeing how he was just as happy to see her as she was to see him. She was now walking in her destiny. Someone was looking out for her after all she'd been through. Meeting Roman had been her saving grace.

She got out of her car and walked over to join everyone at the fair, walking right up to Roman.

"You're here!" Roman said when he turned around and came face to face with Marissa.

"I told you I would be here. Everything looks amazing," she said.

"You look amazing and I'm glad you made it. Things are just about to begin."

"Is there anything I can help with?" she asked.

"I invited you here to enjoy yourself," Roman said.

"I know, but I feel like I should be helping and not just enjoying."

"Then by all means, jump right in."

Marissa turned at the voice behind her and came face to face with a tall, beautiful woman.

"Marissa, this is Pastor Battle. She's pastor of the church here. Pastor, this is Marissa Ballard, a friend of mine."

"Well, hello Marissa and what a beautiful name. We're glad you could make it. I heard you saying you would like to help and we never turn down anyone who wants to pitch in. It's what the community and church are all about. I know Roman has a lot to do, so why don't you come and let me introduce you to the leader of our hospitality ministry who will let you know where we need help."

"That sounds great. It's okay that I'm not a member?" she asked.

"It's perfectly fine. Our church and the work we do isn't about membership. We have lots of people who help out and even work on ministries in the church who are not members. Only those in leadership positions must be members. We want people to feel comfortable with coming or not coming, but knowing we are here and welcome them into the fold in whatever capacity they feel comfortable. When the time comes and they are ready to join, we look forward to helping them get the love and support in ministry that they need. Now, let's see if we can find

Sis. Jackie who can help you get involved."

Marissa waved at Roman who beamed as she walked away.

After introductions were made, Marissa and Jackie were left alone to talk about the places were help was needed. When she saw that there was a need to keeping entertainment in line and on schedule, which included various dancers, she asked about that, sharing her love for dance with Jackie. Though the dancing she'd done wasn't for the church, she loved dancing and could lend her support there the most.

"That would be great," Jackie said. "I'll get you the clipboard of everyone who will be on the stage and the idea is to keep them flowing on and off without much time in in between."

Marissa took the clipboard that was handed to her and glanced over the schedule. She saw that the church had several dance ministries from children, to youth and young adult and even a women's dance ministry. There were also dance ministries for boys and men along with singers, wrappers, steppers and even those who would do mime. She was excited. Anything about entertainment held her interest. She listened as Jackie gave out more instructions and she finally headed toward the tent were lots of children and adults were gathered. As she entered the tent, she looked around and her eyes locked on a familiar face. Standing a few feet ahead of her with a glare on her face was Raquel, a friend from her childhood. She had recently run into Raquel on the street where they had grown up together, only to have Raquel cross to the other side of the street to avoid any contact. Raquel knew about her life and what she'd been up to the past few years while living in New Jersey.

After leaving Philadelphia, Raquel was one person she'd stayed in contact with and in whom she confided in for two years after moving. It was during some of those chats that she felt Raquel pulling away from being the friend she once was to the person criticizing her for leaving her life to become, a stripper, dancing for money for men, showing her body, sometimes all of it, dabbing in drugs and so many other things that raced through her mind the moment they saw each other.

Raquel was standing with three other women who were dressed in dance attire. For several seconds, she couldn't take her eyes from Raquel who didn't even attempt bringing a smile that resembled a greeting to her face. Instead, she leaned over and whispered to the ladies who were with her and they all turned in Marissa's direction, causing her nerves to become jittery. What was Raquel telling them? Whatever it was couldn't be pleasant because they all now had matching looks of repugnance on their faces. They knew her secret and she felt exposed. She looked around for any lifeline and saw none. She didn't have anywhere to go. Trying to ignore them, she moved further into the tent when one of the women walked up to her.

"Can we help you with something?" the woman said.

Marissa cleared her throat and spoke up.

"I've been asked to work in this tent to be sure everyone stays on schedule," she explained calmly even though her nerves were all over the place.

"Is that right? Are you a member here at the church?"

"No, I'm not. I am volunteering to help where I can."

"Really? Are you dancing today? I understand you have a certain dance skill that I'm not sure will fit in with this crowd. We have children here."

Marissa was stunned. This woman she didn't know was outwardly chastising her about something in her past.

"I'm not here to dance. I'm only here to help keep everyone on and off the stage to be sure there is time for everyone."

"Still, you dance though, right? You think that kind of dancing gives you the okay to be around these impressionable children? We don't want them learning the wrong kind of dance. A stripper in the church is disgusting. You don't belong here," she blurted out, causing Marissa to jump back out of fear and hurt.

"Deacon Adams!" Roman said curtly behind Marissa.

"Deacon Hale. I didn't see you standing there," Jackie said.

"Clearly you didn't from what I'm hearing coming out of our mouth. You've said enough! We have a volunteer here and what do you think you're doing? Are those the words of a deacon? Are those the words of someone who should be representing the heart of Christ? How dare you crucify anyone on the spot for something in their past that's none of your business," he countered.

"Well, I was simply looking out for the children. In this day and time, we have to be careful about the character of the people we expose our children to."

Roman was about to reply when Marissa dropped the clipboard and ran toward the parking lot. More important than going back and forth with Jackie, Marissa's stability was his priority as he turned and followed after her, catching up to her at her car.

"Marissa," he said.

"Don't. Did you see the pure hatred in her eyes?

Did you see how those women looked at me like I was trash? I saw her talking with someone I know who must have told her about me being an exotic dancer."

"That's who you were and it's none of her business," he said.

"She made it her business. I shouldn't have come. I told you how I feel about church people. Sometimes, they are worse than the people I meet in everyday life. They think they can dictate how someone lives their lives even when they don't know the whole story. I'm not trash, Roman," she said, beginning to cry.

Roman looked down and saw her hand nervously shaking as she grabbed for the door handle. He covered her shaking hand with his to calm her down and give her his support and love.

"No, you're not. Even then you weren't. You are a beautiful, incredible and have a heart that exudes love. Don't let anyone take that away from you," he said.

"Within the hour, everyone will know because of Raquel."

"Raquel Joyner? You know her?" he asked.

"Yes. I grew up with her. Back then we went to the same church."

"She's a member here now and Jackie is a Deacon and is one of the last people who should ever approach anyone with negativity in the name of this church. That will be dealt with by our ministry chairperson, but for now, I don't want you to leave. Don't let one person be the cause of you running out of here as if you have something to be embarrassed or ashamed about. She was wrong and never should have said those things to you."

"You heard all of it?" she looked up into his eyes and asked.

"I didn't, just the last statement when I stepped in. I saw her talking to you and it didn't look pleasant, so I walked over to see what was going on. She was wrong, but don't let her win. Negativity should never win."

"No, Roman she wasn't wrong. My character will always come into question when people find out about what I've done and trust me, Raquel will tell everyone she can. Clearly, it was meant to make me go away and now they have their wish."

"I wish you wouldn't run away. Aren't you tired of running? If you need a friendly face, I'm here. I invited you because I thought you would have a great time. I'm sorry you were met with such resistance from a leader in the church, in fact. She didn't represent the pastor or this church well and that's not the norm here."

"It's the norm everywhere. Just like my mother won't let me forget and move on, others won't either. That's what's kept me away for so long," she cried softly.

"Don't let it make you run away again. I haven't treated you in any way other than respectful and I always will. I like you, Marissa, something you know. I don't want you to leave here upset like this and thinking that the whole world is judging you."

"Aren't they?" she asked.

"I'm not. Doesn't that count for something?" Roman asked.

Marissa started to continue to plead the case of why she was running away, but couldn't the moment she looked into his consoling face. Roman was right. Since the moment they met, he has shown her nothing, but kindness despite knowing her story. She didn't want to run from him. He was one of the brightest spots in her life right now. His friendship meant everything to her and she didn't want to disappoint him.

"It counts for everything and I'm not running from you. I'm not ready, but that doesn't mean I'm feeling bad about you because I'm not. I'm going to go back to the house and get some things done. Can you just call me later or even stop by before you go to work?"

"You're going to miss Nina seeing Nina dance."

"I know she's going to be beautiful and will dance like an angel. Can I take a raincheck?" she asked and tried to smile to let him know she was going to be okay.

"This isn't the experience I wanted you to have here. I don't want to push you to stay if you'd feel more comfortable leaving. I want to be sure you know I'm in your corner. Are you sure you're okay? I can make sure this all gets cleaned up right now."

Marissa touched his arm lightly.

"Don't. Let it go," she implored.

"Are you sure you're okay?" he asked.

"I'm positive."

To ease his mind, she smiled up at him and when he smiled back, she knew they were going to be okay.

"Okay, drive safe. I'm going to miss seeing you have fun. I will stop by to check on you before I go to work. I'll stop and get us some fattening food," he said, trying to lighten the moment.

"I love that idea. I'll be there waiting. Thanks for being who you are. I guess I'm not ready for people's interaction with me when they know things about me."

"I'm sorry about that encounter," he said somberly.

"I know, but it's not your fault and that kind of chastisement is not my first, last or worst one. I get worse from my mother. I'm fine and I promise, I'm not running away. I'm just going home, okay?"

"Okay and I almost forgot about something I was going to mention to you today. If you're not busy tomorrow, you should come by the house and have dinner with Nina and me. Even though it's November, the temperature is unseasonably warm and I promised her we would have hot dogs and burgers on the grill. Would you come if I texted you the address?" he asked.

His house. He said his house. Roman was asking her over to his house. What does that mean?

"I don't know," she stuttered out.

"Don't think too hard on this. It's just dinner, conversation and maybe a Disney movie because that's the only kind I let Nina watch and she always control the remote. She's learning early that she's in control," he joked.

Marissa laughed, too.

"I'd love to. I'll see you after church tomorrow. Thanks for the invitation to the fair today."

"Sorry about the altercation, but I'm glad you gave it a chance. Rain check on another event?" he asked.

"Most definitely."

Roman kissed her lightly on the cheek and opened the car door for her.

Marissa got in her car and drove away, looking back at Roman standing there. He was turning out to be unlike any man she'd ever met before. He was the kind of man women dreamed of getting attention from and he wasn't asking for anything other than getting to know her and spending time with her. Despite the stories she told him about her life, he didn't judge and was still interested. That was saying something and she wouldn't turn her back on that or him. Maybe her mother would let her take Lacey out for a few hours. She didn't want to go into too many details, afraid her mother would immediately say no. She would explain more when she took Lacey back that evening. She would then tell them about the incredible man Roman was, knowing that he was the opposite of who they thought would be the kind of man who had an interest in her. Probably not, but she was going to try. She had to keep trying to keep her sanity and to get her life back. Her life was Lacey.

15

Roman moved around his kitchen running from the refrigerator to the outside grill, prepping food for dinner. He smiled and hummed a song in his head happy that Marissa was coming over for dinner. Not only was she coming, but he was excited for her when she sent him a text early in the morning as he was getting off work and heading to church letting him know that her mother had agreed to allow her to bring Lacey over for a play date with Nina. He hadn't yet met her family, but she told him that her parents were aware of who he was and her mother didn't have an issue, but Lacey could only be gone for a couple of hours. He wanted to be sure food was ready when they got there instead of cooking once they arrived. He didn't want to waste time cooking when they could make sure the girls had time to play. After service, he came right home and helped Nina clean up her room. He hadn't told her that Lacey was coming, just in case things didn't pan out. She would be excited when they arrived.

"Nina, did you change out of your church clothes? I

left a sweat suit for you to put on along with sneakers and a tshirt in your bathroom," he screamed up the steps. He could hear her moving around in her room.

"Yes, daddy!" she hollered back down to him.

He had been upset the day before when Marissa had pretty much been accosted by a leader of his church, an act he couldn't let go. As soon as he returned to the fair, he went in search of the ministry leader, Deacon Charles, who served over the Deacons and informed him of the behavior of one of their leaders. He was just as upset as Roman had been. An hour later, the pastor came over to him and asked what had occurred. Once he explained what he'd actually heard and what Marissa filled him in on that he'd missed before walking up to them, she was upset and was sad to hear that Marissa was so distraught that she left the fair before it even began. He assured her that Marissa was fine after he talked to her, but still, the pastor was fiery mad, knowing that's not the kind of leader she wants greeting not only visitors, but other members of the church. She let him know that the Deacon Charles was on top of it and that Deacon Jackie would be sat down once all of the facts were on the table and until she'd gone through counseling with the pastor on what it means to have the heart of God when in a leadership position. She looked to them to be the example at all times and Deacon Adams had failed.

Roman was happy to hear that the pastor was just

as upset as he was. He didn't want to think of the number of other members who may have had the same kind of interaction Deacon Jackie that they didn't know about. He didn't tell Marissa that his pastor wanted to talk to her to personally apologize for what happened and to reassure her that the reception she received should not deter her from coming back to the church again. He would bring that up and make sure it was okay that he shared her cell phone number with Pastor Battle. One thing he enjoyed about his church was his pastor didn't allow mess. When she encountered it, she shut it down immediately, as she had done with Deacon Jackie.

Roman was falling hard for Marissa. He hadn't told her because he didn't want to scare her away. They had shared a few intimate kisses and snuggled when they went to the movies or watched television together and he wanted her to know how much she meant to him. First, it was important to him that she felt loved, needed and wanted, all those things she'd never felt from others. He didn't want to be another one of those people. He wanted to love her and with Christ as the foundation, that was the only way they would grow to love each other. He knew that the men in her life didn't have the best impression on her and the one man she thought loved her and gave her a child turned out to only want what she could do to continue to line his pockets. That wasn't love, it was need. It wasn't want, it was use and manipulation. He wanted to offer her love.

He found Marissa to be the kind of sweet, kind-hearted and loving woman he saw himself with in his future. When they were together, it was like they put the rest of the world on mute so that they could have their quality time.

Today's dinner was another big step. Marissa was the first woman he'd brought home to his house or allowed to meet Nina who wasn't just a friend in passing. Marissa was so much more and he was ready for Nina to know.

He reached for his phone when it vibrated on the kitchen counter. He smiled after reading a text from Marissa that she was on her way to pick up Lacey on schedule. He couldn't wait for their evening together eating and enjoying their girls.

**

Marissa exited her car, which she had to park quite a few houses down from her parents' house. She had been floating on air all day after speaking with her mother the evening before about her spending the afternoon with Lacey. To her surprise, her mother said she was okay with it as long as Lacey was fine with it. She heard the reservation in her mother's voice and assumed it was her father who pushed for her time with Lacey.

She'd spent her morning preparing for the visit which included a quick stop at the mall for a few gifts. As she walked toward the house, she noticed a black fancy car with tinted windows was driving slowly about the same pace as she was walking. What she didn't want to do was turn and let them know she noticed them. When the car jerked forward ahead her when she was about three houses away from her parents, she let go of a sigh of relief, not knowing what was going on. Then suddenly the car stopped and out jumped Wayne, an unexpected visitor. She tried to walk fast, but he'd walked ahead of her and cut off any further movement. Marissa had never been more afraid in her life. Her eyes briefly cut to her mother's house and she was glad no one was outside. She had high hopes that he would forget about her and leave her alone. His showing up was the complete opposite of that.

"In a hurry?" Wayne said.

Filled with fright, Marissa didn't respond and then she saw two other men had gotten out of the car and had come up behind her, completely blocking her in.

"Yes, I am," she stammered out. "Please move."

"Is that the first thing you have to say to me after running out on me?" Wayne asked.

"I didn't run out on you. If I remember correctly, you threw me out and I left. I know not to stay where I'm not wanted," she said in defiance.

Wayne laughed and it was so sinister that Marissa's fear went up to a new level.

"Really? You stayed around a lot longer than you were wanted, trust me, but you provided a need that

I'm no longer getting and that's a problem. You were a big money maker for me at that club and things have dropped off. You need to get back to your life in Jersey. I knew you would be here. I waited wondering if you would come back here, but knowing how much your parents hate you, I thought perhaps you were just hiding out from me in New Jersey and then I had a few guys staking out this block and I knew eventually, you may show up and here you are. I've been here scoping out this house for days myself and I never saw you until today. I did see your daughter though. What's her name again? I forget," he said.

Marissa was too scared to be annoyed that he made fun of completely forgetting that Lacey was his daughter, too, though she hated admitting it.

"Stay away from her. You never wanted her."

Wayne laughed and so did his men.

"I still don't. I do want you though, back in Jersey and back on stage. What's with this gear you're sporting? You trying to be normal now or something? Where are the wigs and the face full of makeup? I don't even see much skin, which is odd for you. All you've ever had going for you is this body and yet, you're barely showing it. You can change your clothes, but you're still the same attention seeking, pole dancing tramp and you being here is affecting my money. That's a major problem and I'm not happy. You know what happens when I'm not happy, right?" he leaned down and whispered in her ear.

Wayne's closeness caused her stomach to churn. She wanted away from him.

"I'm not going back to Jersey. I need to be a mother to my daughter and I'm trying to work on myself," she admitted.

"Work on yourself? What is that supposed to mean? You are what you are and we both know what that is? You shake this money maker and the dollar bills drop in piles around your feet. This is my money you're messing with and I can't let you walk away from that. I could walk up to that house and introduce myself to my daughter and see where that gets me. It may be time she met her dear ol' dad, don't you think?" he asked.

Marissa's skin crawled with every word that slithered of Wayne's mouth and the last thing she wanted was for him to have any interaction with her parents or Lacey.

"Did you really think you were going to get away and stay away? I have more years of big dollars I can get out of you and then we'll move on to some other big time, big dollar amount stuff."

"I'm not going back. My life is here now," Marissa said as she calculated how to get away from Wayne unscathed. She thought back to times of pure torture and physical abuse and she was never going back to that. Then her thoughts turned to Lacey and she knew that the choice was either her or it was Lacey being exposed to Wayne and she couldn't have that.

"No? Are you sure about that? Okay, then let's walk together up the steps to your mother's house and I want them to know I want my daughter!" he demanded.

"You can't have her!" Marissa shouted a little louder than she'd planned.

"Is that what you think? She's mine, isn't she? I don't care who has been raising her, she's still mine and either you come back to Jersey and do what you do best or you and your daughter are coming back to Jersey and I don't care if I have to drag you both out of that house, down the steps and into my car. I don't want to hurt you, your parents or that little girl, so don't make me. Get back in your car and let's go!" Wayne demanded. "Speaking of cars, where is my car? Where is my BMW?"

"I sold it to get a car I could afford to have."

"Is that so. So, you needed that flash before, but not now? Next time I'll know not to put a car in your name. Let's go, Delilah."

Marissa huffed and looked down at the ground.

"Don't call me that," she said and began to cry.

Wayne walked up and stood as close to her as he could get before leaning down so that their faces were right in front of each other.

"You're not in a position to tell me what to do. Now, you can either get in your car and follow me back to Jersey, I can have my guys drag you to my car and throw you in the trunk for the ride back or we can go inside that house up there and I will drag my daughter out of that house by her hair. The choice is yours and you know I'm not joking. Move quickly," he demanded.

Not having a choice, Marissa took one last look at the house and turned around, walking toward her car. She didn't know what else to do. Her first inclination was to protect Lacey and her parents. She couldn't drag them into this life and she knew Wayne was serious. He would have no qualms about dragging Lacey out of the house kicking and screaming. She couldn't let that happen. Before getting the driver's side door open, Wayne walked up to her.

"No detours."

"I need to get my things from my place. I left a lot of money there," she lied, hoping it would buy her a little time. She had to think of something to do to avoid driving straight to Jersey. She needed time to figure out a plan.

"Money? Let's get that money and then we're on the road. Get in and we'll follow you."

Marissa didn't respond. She got in the car and started it up. When she got to the end of the block, she dialed Roman's number the only person she could think of to help her. If anyone could rescue her or tell her a way to get herself out of this predicament, he would."

"Call Roman," she said into the car speaker and the number began to ring.

"Are you almost here?" Roman asked the minute he answered. She knew he would see her number. She couldn't get any words out and instead, she broke out into a loud, uncontrollable cry.

"Marissa? Sweetheart, what's wrong? Marissa!" Roman called again.

"Help me," she mumbled out while checking her rearview mirror to be sure Wayne and his goons couldn't see her talking on the phone.

"What's wrong? You're scaring me. Talk to me," he said quickly.

"Wayne. Wayne showed up at my parents' house and demanded I go back to Jersey with him or he was going to go in their house and take Lacey out and take her away to Jersey."

"Where are you? I'm on my way," he hurriedly said.

"I'm heading back to the house. I don't know where else to go. I told him I had a lot of money there that I needed to get and I knew that would interest him. Anything dealing with money is his priority. I'm not really going there, but I had to tell him something. I don't know what to do. They're following me. He was going to hurt Lacey or my parents. I don't know what to do," she cried.

"Listen to me. I'm going to give you an address to put in your GPS. It's going to take you to a house we use as a witness stash house. No one is there, but by the time you get there, I'll be there with help. Drive slowly if you can without them noticing. If you see a light about to change, get caught behind it. I'm going to take Nina next door and I'm on my way. Keep this line open. I'm going to use my work phone to call for some help. I don't want them tipped off. Whatever you do, don't get out of that car and don't stop. Just drive. Do you understand me. Do not get out of that car. How much gas do you have?" he asked.

After checking, Marissa sighed with relief.

"The tank is full. I have plenty."

"Good. Just drive sweetheart and I'm on my way. Do not get out of the car and you'll be fine. Trust me," he said.

"I trust you. Only you, I trust you."

**

Roman called his neighbor while keeping his other phone on mute and connected to Marissa so that he could hear everything that was going on. After sending Nina next door, he ran to the garage, jumped in his truck and sped off while dialing the precinct. When he got the operator, he was passed to his captain, telling him everything. As he suspected, his captain got men in motion in unmarked police cars to not make themselves known until they were up on the car Wayne was in.

"Hold on one second," he told his captain.

"Marissa, what kind of car are they in?"

After getting the details, Roman relayed the information to his captain and hung up. Things were in motion, but his main concern was getting to

Marissa whom he knew was scared out of her mind. When he first heard her cry, which actually sounded more like a wail, he knew something was wrong and now he knew what.

He hated men who disrespected, mistreated and abused women. If Wayne thought he was leaving Philly with Marissa, he needed to think again. Following the route he gave Marissa, Roman made a few turns right and left and ran one light after the other, not caring about speedlight or red-light cameras. His heart sped up when he turned and ended up a few cars behind the car Marissa told him Wayne was in. He could see her car driving slowly in front of the black car with tinted windows. He kept his distance until he saw the support pulling up.

"I'm behind you. Don't look around, just keep driving," he said in his phone to Marissa. "There are cars that will be pulling up soon. You are only a few blocks from the address I gave you. When you get there, do not get out of the car for any reason. When I tell you to, drive off and go to my house. Don't stop anywhere. Pull up to the garage and wait for me. Understand?" he asked.

"Yes. What about you?" she asked.

"I'm going to be fine."

"I'm scared. I don't want you to get hurt because of me."

"Don't worry about that. I've got this covered. This isn't my first rodeo with men like Wayne. I'll take care of this. You get out of there when I say drive. I don't want you anywhere around when this goes down. I'll be there shortly."

"Okay, be careful. I'm sorry for dragging you into this."

"We're in this together. We haven't talked about what's happening between us, but know that we're in this together."

"Thank you for being you, Roman."

"I'll see you soon."

The moment they all turned onto the street where the house was, Roman noticed three unmarked cars waiting for them. He signaled that he saw them. As soon as Marissa pulled up to the house, the men moved in and surrounded the car that Wayne was in. He then told Marissa to drive off and the minute she was out of harm's way, he jumped out of his car, pulled his badge out of his shirt so that it dangled around his neck and he pulled out his weapon. Everything happened quickly. Everyone screamed at Wayne and the other men to get out of the car and at first, Roman wasn't sure they were going to abide by the instruction which meant things could turn bad. Seconds later, the doors opened and one at a time, four men exited the car and turned with their hands on the roof. He then moved to take over and started with Wayne.

"Hands behind your back," he said loud enough for everyone to hear.

"Man, what is this? What are we being pulled over for? We weren't doing anything," he yelled while also struggling with Roman's hold.

"Go ahead and struggle against me. I want you to. Give me one reason, that's all I need, just one good reason. You like threatening women and their children, Wayne?" he asked, startling Wayne when he said his name. When Wayne tried to look back at him, he shoved his face back down into the car, showing no mercy.

"Man, what are you talking about? I'm not threatening anyone and how do you know my name? She called the police on me? That..."

"Don't even utter it. You won't like my response if you call my woman out of her name," Roman said.

"Your woman? Who are you?"

"Don't worry about that. You need to worry about me right now and how much I hate men who put their hands on a woman or threaten an innocent child with body harm. I don't know where you hail from, but here in the city of brotherly love, we don't take kindly to men to hurt or even threaten to hurt women and children. Keep struggling and I'm going to forget I'm a cop," Roman threatened.

When Wayne stopped struggling, Roman was actually disappointed. He wanted a reason for at least one good punch, but he wouldn't cross the line. He had a feeling there was enough in Wayne's past that the law would be sufficient in dealing with him.

"You got this?" one of the other officer's said to him.

"I got this. Let's run everybody's information and then let's get a look at this car. We have enough to take a look based on the call we received about a woman feeling like her life was in danger with a car full of goons following her, threatening her and forcing her to leave the state. Any of you have a four-legged officer with you? I think we may need to check this car out. I got a feeling," Roman said as he continued to check Wayne and smiling when he came up with a concealed weapon.

"Hey, this is illegal. You don't have any proof I did anything. This search is illegal," Wayne shouted.

"We found weapons on the other three also," one of the other plain clothes officers said.

"Threats against women, weapons and who knows what we'll find in the car," Roman said. He looked around as a swarm of police cars with lights and sirens blaring joined them.

"Car one has one. We need Sal," the officer yelled and another one ran to his car and in an instant, a four-legged shepherd who was a member of the force exited the car. As soon as he got close to the car, he went crazy jumping and barking, letting them know there was something in the car.

Roman chuckled knowing Marissa wouldn't have to worry about him anymore.

"Got something in here?" he asked Wayne. "No

need to answer. We have cause to check. You should have stayed in Jersey," Roman said. "This isn't your day. You should have taken any road except the one that led you here," he added.

"We got a huge bust here, guys!" one of the officers chimed.

Wayne turned and watched them pulled blocks of drugs that were imbedded in the frame of the car.

"You just made my day," Roman said and walked Wayne over to the police van. "Like I said, this isn't your day and lucky for you, I'm not only a police officer, but I'm a man of God or I'd find an abandoned warehouse and show you what I really think about men who abuse women. I'll settle for what the law will throw your way with what we've found," Roman said.

His thoughts turned to Marissa. He needed to get to her to make sure she was okay. He walked back toward his car and dialed her number as he walked.

16

With three weeks behind them since Marissa's encounter with Wayne, Roman observed her playing and replaying that day over and over in her mind because even though she had some good days, it was days like today, on Thanksgiving where even though they were at his parents' house with lots of family around having a good time, she couldn't seem to enjoy herself and that bothered him. Since then, she had been depressed because she'd been unable to see Lacey after everything had gone down and come out. There was no getting around telling her parents about it and they were furious with her, once again, shutting her out of their lives.

After not showing up to pick up Lacey because of what happened, even an explanation didn't satisfy her mother and she'd kept Marissa from Lacey and even her father wasn't in her corner this time. They had equally scolded her about what could have happened and that it was her fault for bringing a dangerous man into their lives. It was hard to think about what could have happened if Wayne had really decided to take Lacey away that day. Her parents were upset, but it was her mother who had the most upsetting response. Besides the events that occurred that day, her mother let her know how disappointed Lacey had been that she'd never shown up. They understood why, but had no plans of explaining that to their granddaughter. Marissa had talked to her on the phone, but had not seen her. He was glad he could convince her to join him and his family for Thanksgiving dinner. They had been there for a few hours and though his family was as gracious as they always were and tried to engage Marissa in conversation, she smiled and responded, but it only lasted a brief moment before she focused on what was in her head, her own family. He smiled at her when his mother invited her to join others in the kitchen and while doing so, he took to his favorite chair next to his father as they watched sports. His eyes were on the game, but his mind was on Marissa and the after effects of the havoc Wayne brought to her life. She felt like she would never be free of him, but he knew differently. There was a lot that went down following his arrest that he looked forward to sharing with her in hopes of easing her mind that he won't be coming back to bother her again.

After a large number of drugs were discovered sealed in various parts of the car and since the car was owned by Wayne, they were all arrested, but Wayne would eventually end up with the shortest end of the stick. The large quantity and the dollar value meant he would be going to jail for a long time and that's in addition to other charges they found were pending for him in New Jersey. Despite the negatives, there were some positive things that occurred over the past few weeks that he was able to celebrate with her and some days, he even had a hand in making her smile.

To his delight, one day out of the blue in the week following Wayne's arrest, Marissa approached him about visiting his church. He was more than excited. From the start, he pictured them in worship together.

Two weeks ago, she joined him for her first service at his church and to his delight, she enjoyed herself. After worship, she met with the pastor who wanted to know if her second experience was a better one. They talked for over an hour and when Marissa came out of the office, his pastor was intrigued by Marissa's work at a law firm as an administrative assistant, a job she'd only held for the past week, but loved. Pastor Battle had mentioned that they were looking for someone to work in the church office two days a week for a few hours and if Marissa was interested, she should stop by and meet the staff. She did and even offered to work her first week as a volunteer so that the staff could see if she fit in. She more than fit in and now she had two jobs where as a few weeks ago, she didn't have one and a few months ago, she had no prospects, not even a place to live. She started to believe God's word that He would never leave her. He brought her through and was still championing for her.

He loved that Marissa was now spending just as much time at the church as he was. Over the weekend, she'd joined the women's dance ministry and had attended her first rehearsal where she again ran into Raquel who still didn't speak or acknowledge Marissa, but that was okay. Marissa was stronger in her determination to not fail and fall back to a life where she wasn't happy.

Hearing his mother call out that dinner was ready, he joined the rest of the family around the table. Sitting next to Marissa at the dinner table had him feeling nostalgic and longing for more days like this with Marissa being treated like a member of the family. "Marissa, you have to eat more than that," his mother said from across the table. Roman could see that he wasn't the only one who noticed Marissa's lack of interest in food.

"She's trying to keep her figure, mom," Roman's sister Sherry said which did get a slight smile from Marissa. The two of them were already developing a connection after he'd introduced her to Marissa two weeks ago at his house. This was the first time she was meeting his parents and other extended family. Everyone welcomed Marissa as if they'd known her for years. Roman had no doubt that would happen. He has the kind of family who led by their hearts. They were all excited knowing Roman had never invited a woman to any holiday function in many years, not since Melanie. Even if he didn't realize it, everyone realized something very poignant. He was head over heels in love with Marissa. Oh, he knew it, but he hadn't said it out loud to anyone. Nina loved being around her and often asked about Lacey. She got to see her at story time, but Nina noticed that Marissa never came around with Lacey. Roman had to talk to her about that so that she didn't keep digging deeper with question after question. He told her when Marissa was ready, she would bring Lacey around. He hoped one day, their daughters could bond.

Roman concentrated on eating and contemplated what he would say to her on the ride back to her house after dinner. She had a hand in bringing his heart back to life and he would do anything to see her in a happier place every day.

**

"Martika, you outdid yourself this year with dinner. Everything was delicious and I could tell by the smiles on everyone's face that they enjoyed it as well.

William leaned back in his black leather recliner in the living room as she entered, drying her hands on a Thanksgiving themed hand towel and sat in the matching chair next to his.

"I'm glad you enjoyed it. I think this was our best year yet. We've never had this much family over for a holiday meal. I forgot how large our family was. Where's Lacey? I thought I heard her in here watching television and singing Disney songs," Martika said.

William grunted and shifted in his seat. He'd been

thinking about having a talk with his wife for a few days and especially now, after dinner with everyone gone home. The minute she mentioned their granddaughter, his thoughts turned to her and how unhappy she'd been, not just at dinner, but for the past few weeks.

Lacey had come to him asking about her mother and he tried to explain to her that there were some problems and he hoped she'd be able to see Marissa soon. He didn't know what else to say. For years, he'd allowed his wife to dictate the kind of relationship or the lack of one that they'd had with their daughter, but this year had been a struggle for him. He could see his daughter was trying and even though he'd been angry hearing about Lacey's father causing trouble outside of their house, after his initial anger, he knew it wasn't Marissa's fault, but he was upset. He now realized his reaction was exactly what Martika needed to pour more gasoline on an already fueled situation when it came to Marissa. For the first time, he was able to look into his granddaughter's eyes and see the impact of their treatment of Marissa and he didn't like it. He turned his body all the way around to face Martika.

"She went to bed. She was tired, so I told her to get her bath, get her pajamas on and she ran back down after doing that and gave me a hug and then ran back upstairs," he replied.

"Without coming into the kitchen to say goodnight

to me?" Martika asked, surprised.

William reached for the remote and turned off the television.

"You know, I complimented you on dinner tonight and I meant that and the fact that we had lots of family here for the holiday was great. You and I both know what was missing and Lacey did as well," he said.

"Marissa," Martika answered before leaning back and exhaling her impatience.

"Lacey is older now and she feels the tension. Things were different when Marissa was just gone and we didn't hear from her except for the occasional phone call. With her being back in town, hiding displeasure with Marissa is harder to do and Lacey is feeling the impact. Can't you see that?" he asked.

"See what? Marissa screwed up and you know it. Do you know how much danger she could have put us and Lacey in having that man here at our house? He was trash when she met him and he's still trash. I'm glad he's where he belongs, behind bars. The hope is that he'll be there for a long time."

"True and the sad part is that we had to hear the latest on the evening news like everyone else and not from our daughter first-hand. We're losing her again and you don't seem to care. That's not the woman with the big heart that I married and pledged to love forever. That's not the woman I had a child with and who should be loving her unconditionally like she loves everyone else's child at the church. It bothers me that you treat others better than you treat your own child."

"I have never said I don't love Marissa. I do love her, but I can't hide my disappointment in how she lives her life."

"It's her life and all we can do is be here for her, not push her further away with anger. True, she picked the wrong guy and it appears we won't have to worry about him anymore."

"That's a big blessing in all of this," Martika exclaimed.

"Right and what about Marissa? I don't know that man and I'm glad I don't, but Marissa is our daughter and this has gone on long enough."

"What do you expect me to do? Risk her bringing harm to Lacey? Never!" she shouted.

"Keep your voice down before Lacey hears you. I think she's heard too much already. You don't know this, but after she came to tell me good night, I told her not to forget to give you a hug and a kiss and when she walked away, I caught her movement from the corner of my eye. I watched her hesitate at the stairs and she was thinking about whether to go in the kitchen or not. She chose not to and she ran up the stairs, almost like she was tiptoeing so you wouldn't hear her."

Martika gasped in shock.

"Why would she do that? I'll just march upstairs

and ask her."

"You will not!" he shouted.

William shocked himself. He'd never shouted at his wife before, but this cycle of damaged relationships was not going to continue with their granddaughter or with their daughter any longer.

"Why not?" she asked.

"She's heard you talking about Marissa and not in a nice way. I didn't want to tell you this because it was Thanksgiving, but a few days ago while I was driving her home from school, she asked my why you didn't like her mother, why you hated her. I told her that wasn't true and I asked her why she would think such a thing and she said that she could hear you being mean to Marissa on the phone sometimes and that she heard you tell her that she was a terrible mother to choose her own life over a better life with her daughter. What were you thinking having a phone conversation like that with Lacey in the house? She's not an infant anymore. She's a curious six-year-old and she's paying attention even when we don't think she is."

"I didn't mean for her to hear that. Marissa made me so angry, demanding to see Lacey as if she has any right."

"Martika, she is Lacey's mother and she has every right. I've gone along with this treatment of our daughter for so long, I've become immune to it. She should have been here today and our granddaughter wouldn't have had to look toward the door in anticipation every time someone rang the doorbell only to be let down when it wasn't her mother. She moped around here all day and you never even noticed," he said.

"I had a house full of guests," she tried to explain.

"Guests or not, you should have noticed how unhappy Lacey has been these past few weeks, especially today and even if she doesn't say it, her mother not being here or even coming around anymore is your fault and she doesn't know how to process loving you and loving her mother whom you are choosing not to show love for."

"What do you want me to do, William? We have to protect Lacey. You know what Marissa's life has been like, what she's been doing and the kind of people she's been around. You can't possibly want that for Lacey," she said, defiantly.

"No, I don't, but I don't want to see Lacey unhappy either. There has to be a compromise."

William stood and headed for the stairs.

"We've tried compromising and look what it brought us. Some lunatic showing up at our house threatening to take Lacey," Martika rebuked.

William didn't face her when he reached the steps. Instead, he kept his eyes on those twelve steps that led to the upstairs landing.

"Marissa should have been here today. I was angry at her too, but then I looked at everyone who was here and I don't know what I've been feeling over the years, but today, I missed my daughter. She's right here in Philadelphia, a phone call away and she wasn't invited to spend the holidays with her family. She may be someplace all alone, not having anyone to eat with and share in family times with and here we are celebrating a bunch of people who don't even pay us much mind until we're having them over for a free meal. No one asked about her and no one missed her, but me and Lacey. It has to stop. I'm getting older and so are you. We have missed good years with her and I don't care what she's done. You can stop harping on that because it's old and tired to do so. I'm tired of this Martika and we have to do better, not just you. Together, we must do better if for no other reason than to make sure Lacey knows, loves and has a good relationship with her mother. Don't turn her and Marissa into you and Marissa. We go to church every Sunday. We serve as Deacons, we serve on the Intercessory Prayer Ministry, you work with the Helping Hands Ministry, helping young women who need guidance and counseling in order to make a better life for themselves and their children and I have no doubt God smiles on you for the work you do. Yet, here you are, persecuting your own daughter, not offering to help her, not praying for her or trying to help her rejoin this family where she belongs. We call ourselves Christians and we've done the right thing by raising our granddaughter, but I don't think God is pleased with how we're handling Marissa. I don't think he is. Our daughter has been crying out for help for a lot of years, even many before she left here and didn't return until she had Lacey in her arms as an infant. I'm ashamed to say I did nothing and I'm more ashamed that even now, I'm still doing nothing and neither are you. We're not thinking about Lacey. We're not being Christ-like in how we treat our own daughter. We need someone to counsel us, pray for us and help us find a path to a better life. We're failing as parents and as Christians. I love my granddaughter and I love my daughter, just as much as I love you, but this isn't right. Lacey is hurting and you're still trying to be angry at Marissa. I'm going upstairs and I'm going to pray that God will soften your heart and that He'll forgive us both for this two-faced Christian life we're living. I'm going to kiss my granddaughter and apologize for my role in her not having a relationship with her mother."

William didn't wait for Martika to have any more say in the matter. He swiftly ascended the stairs and began his prayer as he walked, not praying silently, but out loud so that his wife could hear his every word. He started by asking God for forgiveness for his house.

**

Roman drove as he and Marissa rode in silence. They'd just left his parents' house and with Nina fast asleep in the back seat, he was happy to have a few minutes to talk.

"I'm sorry you're sad today. I wanted to put a smile on your face by asking you to join my family for dinner," he said looking her way, although her eyes were focused on what was on the outside of the car as they drove by.

He wasn't sure she'd heard him until he was about to continue and she turned around.

"There is nothing for you to apologize for. I had a wonderful time with your family. I know I had already met your sister when she was at your house and the rest of your family was so nice to me, especially your mother. She really went out of her way to make me feel comfortable," Marissa said.

"That's definitely my mother," he said.

"That's also you. Thank you for being you. You, Lacey and Nina are the brightest parts of my life. I also have the people at the church, too and that's some comfort," she admitted.

"It's not enough though, right?" he asked.

Marissa hesitated and tried to look away.

"I'm sorry," she said softly.

"Don't look away and don't look down in defeat. Keep your head up. You've been doing so much better."

"Not good enough for my parents. It's Thanksgiving and they didn't even care that I could have been alone today. If it wasn't for you and your family, I would have been."

"You're not alone."

"Do you know that my whole life, my parents have been about church, day and night. They are officers, like you. They are proud to call themselves missionaries, yet I'm the one person they can't seem to open their hearts to. How can that be? How can God play such a cruel trick?"

"This isn't God's fault. I know your parents love you and there have been some issues, but none of them have anything to do with love. They have been disappointed, yes, hurt, probably, but they still love you enough to look after Lacey and in time, they will come around."

"I'm thankful I have you."

Roman chuckled.

"That day we met and how we met, I think about all the time. Never have I ever found myself thinking about someone I met while on duty, but something about you stuck with me and then strangely enough, I ran into you later that day. It had to be fate and not coincidence. You've brought so much life into my life. I had been down on my own self and meeting and getting to know you has given me new life. Even Nina told me she can tell I smile more now."

"I like your smile," Marissa said and smiled.

"Just my smile?" he questioned.

"No. I like you, too."

"You already know it's mutual. I don't want to lose what we've been gaining. I don't know where it's leading, but I like the feeling that it is leading somewhere."

"I do, too. If it wasn't for you, I probably would have been back in Jersey by now, giving up on a better life."

"Then I'd say whatever God's plan is for our lives, we are walking in that destiny. I don't want you to give up. I would do anything to keep a smile on your face. You once told me in passing that you once screamed for God to help you, to rescue you and He did, even when you didn't know He was working for your good. He still is, even on days like today when you miss your family and wished they missed you. Things will continue to turn around and only good will come out of it. Just don't give up, not on your family and not on us."

Roman reached his hand across the middle console of the car and when Marissa moved her hand toward his, he grabbed it, brought her hand to his lips and kissed the back of it before leaning over when they reached the next light and kissing her lovingly. When the light changed, they pulled away so that he could drive, but he drove in happiness, enjoying the feel on her lips where they had connected with his.

When Marissa leaned back and closed her eyes as they drove, his mind was on her parents. He could feel God at work and He was giving him a new assignment.

17

Roman walked up the steps to Marissa's parents' house hoping he would be able to catch them at home. After Thanksgiving, he'd let a week go by before getting up the nerve, after much prayer, to speak to them. He may not have known Marissa for a long time, but the woman he now knew was giving her all into being a better person and to his dismay, her family was the last hurdle to her coming full circle in life and realizing she can walk through life with her head up without shame.

He waited as long as he could before making the decision to visit the Ballards. He'd prayed and then prayed some more that God would deliver the words he needed to speak to explain to her parents the mistake they were making in not working harder to mend the broken relationship with Marissa. There were days that he wished he could have his wife back so that she could have an unbreakable bond with Nina, but that wasn't to be and he relegated himself to the fact that God knew best and he no longer questioned it. At one time, he thought that Melanie was the only love he'd ever have, but now he knew that God had brought Marissa into his life to show him that love doesn't die with the dead. It thrives and the heart will heal in order to love again. God showed him someone who was hurting more than he was and then he could no longer focus on his small hurt when Marissa had larger, more damaging hurts and she needed a friend. She needed someone who was willing to be patient with her and understand her imperfections, yet still know that her imperfections are what made her the perfect person. He wanted his relationship with Marissa to continue to grow, but first he had to say his peace and hope her parents would appreciate where he was coming from and how much Marissa misses them and needs them and their love in her life.

Most importantly, Marissa needs time with her daughter. He knew she was growing more frustrated with each passing day with no physical contact with Lacey. He had to find a way to fix that and all he could think about was talking to her parents. He didn't tell Marissa he was coming or she probably would have tried to stop him. The God in him had to do something.

Ringing the doorbell, he waited and silently prayed that he would find understanding on the other side of the door. He hoped he didn't appear intimidating since he was still in his uniform having just gotten off from work. He knew that their treatment of Marissa was wrong and if they wouldn't listen to how she's changed from her own lips, perhaps they would listen to him. Who wouldn't listen to the words of a police officer?

On his break, he'd driven through their block several times before deciding to get out of his patrol car. There was no turning back now, he thought as the front door finally opened and a gentleman, he assumed was Marissa's father looked at him questionably.

"Good evening, sir," he said. Before he could say anything else, her father interrupted.

"What happened? Is something wrong? Did something happen to someone?" William asked.

Roman knew he needed to calm her father's immediate agitation at seeing him at his door and in uniform. Usually when that occurred, that meant something unpleasant had happened and an officer was delivering the news.

"No sir, it's nothing like that. I'd like to talk to you about Marissa," he said and waited for some kind of reaction.

"Marissa?" Martika asked joining them at the door. "What has she done now? Is she in legal trouble?" she added.

"Is Marissa okay or is she hurt?" William asked, dismissing Martika's response to their visitor.

"Yes, sir, she's fine. Do you mind if I come in and speak to you for a few minutes? I promise you she hasn't done anything wrong, she's not injured or anything else that would cause you any grief. This is actually a friendly visit, if that's possible at seven in the evening."

"Come on in," William said.

Roman walked in after the invitation and waited to be invited to sit.

"Thank you for allowing me some of your time to talk."

"What's happened to her?" Martika asked as they walked into the living room.

"Nothing's happened to her, ma'am."

"Well, I assumed if the police showed up at the door talking about Marissa, she's in some kind of trouble again," she said.

"He said nothing was wrong," William said.

"Yes, nothing is wrong and I'm sorry for not properly introducing myself. My name is Roman Hale and I'm a friend of your daughter's. I'm not here in a legal capacity," Roman said.

"I'm William and this is my wife, Martika."

"It's nice to meet you both."

"Likewise," they said together.

Roman accepted Martika's extended handshake and smiled.

"Mr. Hale, you said you're here about Marissa?" William asked.

"Yes, and please call me, Roman, sir." He turned and sat when William pointed to a chair.

"Well, if you're not here because something has happened to Marissa, what's the reason for the visit? I know you said you were friends with Marissa. We didn't know she had any friends who were police. Over the years, she has had another type of interaction with police and visits from them haven't been friendly," Martika said.

"I understand that. Marissa has shared her past with me, but I assure you, I'm not here for anything that would bring bad news."

"Then why are you here?" William questioned.

"Well, as I stated, I am a friend of Marissa's and I'm actually here on her behalf, but she doesn't know it. I don't want to take up too much of your time, so here it is. I know that Marissa has a past, but that's not who she is now. She told me she's reached out to you several times to work on things with you and with her daughter and she feels like she's not getting anywhere because you won't allow her to get beyond her past."

Roman could see they were anxious to counter what he was saying.

"I'm not sure we should be talking about this without her here," William said.

"With all due respect, I think this is the perfect time to talk about it and if you would have allowed her here, maybe you could have talked about this. She's hurting and she's broken. I know there have been issues over the years and most recently the problem with Wayne, which myself and other officers quickly dealt with when she called me."

"She called you?" William asked.

"Yes. She called me from the car. She told me she was in trouble and what was going on and that she did what she had to do in order to keep him away from your house. She put herself in danger to protect you."

"We didn't know about that. She told us what happened that day, but she didn't say anything about deflecting danger from us by putting herself in harm's way," William added.

Again, with all due respect, you haven't given her a real chance to explain. Marissa has been working hard at overcoming the things she's done that sent her to the lowest points in her life, but she's slowly climbing out of that. I won't go into the circumstances of how I met her, but let me say that I was having my own inner struggles with a few things and before her, I was hesitant to talk to anyone about them. I went through a very hard time in my life a few years ago and I can't imagine what my life would have been like if it weren't for my mother and father supporting me and being there just to listen when I needed to vent. I've been that person for Marissa and we've brought each other out of those dark places that were consuming us. Our problems were different, but we were in the same place of not knowing what to do and how to be an overcomer. Together, we have found our strength, but my heart bleeds for Marissa because she loves and misses you, especially Lacey. She was just getting to a happy place in her life with Lacey and then the rug was pulled from under her when you wouldn't allow her to see Lacey. I care a great deal for your daughter and I want what's best for her and that is to work things out with you and to be able to spend time with Lacey."

"I've had several calls with Marissa and I could tell she was a different person," William said. "I've missed her so much and I know Lacey has missed her," he added.

"I came here to ask or rather beg you to please let Marissa into your hearts and into your lives again. She's really trying to make amends for the things she's done and her first step was to walk away from the life she was living. She's trying to find her way, but I don't think she'll find it without your love," he said.

Roman watched as William looked down at his hands which were trembling, then over at his wife as she reached out and grasped his hand in hers. He hoped he was getting through to them because he knew that the steps Marissa had already taken were shaky and could only be sealed and made sturdy with the love and support of her parents.

"We have been hard on Marissa and that's out of disappointment for what she had done to her life and to the life of her daughter. It's been hard on us all, but out of anger, I never stopped to think of how hard things were for Marissa. I looked at it as a choice she made when her options were in front of her face. It hurt that she chose that life over a life here with us and her daughter," Martika said.

"Marissa feels that hurt from you every single day. Each time she's reached out to you lately, she comes away with an even deeper hurt. If you would find it in your heart to give her a chance, I think you'll see that she's changed. She moved back to Philadelphia to be closer to you and Lacey. She told me how she was brought up in the church and how she turned her back on it when she met up with an un-seedy person. She faults herself for getting caught up and every day, she beats herself up more and more. She needs you; she needs Lacey. She's working and doing wonderful now that she's back in Philly. She also spends time at church and even works in the church office as part of the administrative team two days a week. She's on the dance ministry and is also beginning to work with the children's dance ministry where my own daughter is a member. She wants and needs to make amends, not just as an apology to you, but so that she can look forward to a future that is hopefully filled with family and love."

"Roman, are you in love with Marissa?" Martika asked.

"Yes, ma'am – I am," he admitted.

The love he felt for her had started growing in his heart not long after he'd met her and it grew stronger with each day. He loved the woman he'd come to know over the past few months.

"I never would have thought...." Martika started then stopped.

"It's okay because when I met her, I never thought I'd feel the kind of love for her that I do," Roman admitted.

"You said she's been going to church?" Martika asked.

"Yes. She's been coming, pretty regularly now for the past month to my church, Brownstone Gospel Fellowship Church," Roman said.

"That's Pastor Lorenda Battle's church, I believe. She's preached several times at our church. She's a dynamic preacher and a true woman of God," William said.

"That she is and she's been a great help to Marissa in helping her mend and grow."

"Marissa had turned her back on the church for so many years," Martika said.

"True, she had and that was because she doesn't think she's worthy of His love because she's lost your love, the two people she's loved most in her life before Lacey came along. I can tell her she's worthy and loved every single day, but it's your love that she seeks the most. I think that will help her heal and let herself off of the hook for her past. She works at the church, she also works as an assistant at a law firm and she's taking classes two evenings a week. Marissa is making great strides and is happier, but there is still a sadness that I can't wash away."

"Wow, we had no idea she was doing all that."

"She has and I'm there to support her to make sure she continues to thrive. She hopes to move into her own apartment soon and she's actually saving up so that she can afford a place where there would be a room for Lacey, that is if you allow her visits. She doesn't want to go back to her old life and she's trying to forget about it and leave it in her past. She can only do that if you're willing to do that, too. I can't tell you what to do, but please reconsider allowing her to spend time with Lacey."

"Is it your house she was going to that day for a play date with your daughter?" Martika asked.

"Yes. I know she wasn't specific about that, but yes, our daughters are the same age and have shared in some of the same extracurricular activities."

"I think I've seen you at Lacey's cheerleading practice and at some of the story times," William stated.

"Yes, sir, I think you have. My daughter loves cheerleading and she met Lacey there."

"Isn't that something that you also met Marissa. It's a small world," Martika said.

"Yes, and it's even smaller without family in your corner. Listen, I don't want to take up too much of your time."

Roman pulled a flyer from his pocket, unfolded it and handed it to them.

"What's this?" Martika asked.

"It's a holiday festival at my church where Marissa is going to not only show what she's been teaching the children dancers, but she's also going to do a solo dance performance. It's in three weeks, right before Christmas," Roman said.

"In church?" Martika asked.

"Yes, in church. I am hoping that you will consider coming and bringing Lacey with you. Marissa doesn't know I'm here, but I will tell her that I stopped by to talk to you and that I offered you an invitation to the program. It's time for your family to heal because without you, Marissa won't survive for the long haul. She needs you in her life."

Roman stood to leave.

"I'm glad you came by," William said, taking his hand in a handshake.

"I'm glad I was able to meet you. I'm going to leave you with what we talked about and I pray that you'll consider joining us in worship and also that you'll reconsider and let Marissa into your hearts. She loves you," he said.

"We love her, too," William added.

Roman noticed Martika didn't say anything and when he looked her way, she was still sitting while holding her head in her hands. He let her be.

"I hope to see you again soon," he said to William who opened the door for him.

"It was nice meeting you and I'm glad you stopped by. I think your visit is exactly what my wife needed.

She was close, but I think your visit and your love for our daughter did what God sent you here to do. Thank you and we'll see about this program."

Roman nodded his head and left. As he walked to his car, he felt hopeful that he was able to get through to them. Marissa's future depended on it.

18

Marissa checked herself in the full-length mirror to be sure she was presentable. She had spent many years dancing for the wrong reason and for the wrong audiences. She was thankful for the change in venue and the opportunity to get her life back on track. She lowered her head and closed her eyes.

"God, it's me, Marissa. I know by now you're tired of the back and forth with me. I'm making you work overtime. I'm sorry for my short lapse in judgement. I'm still having a hard time understanding the gap that still exists with my family, but I'm trusting you and putting the situation totally in your hands. I want to thank you for all that you've done and all that you'll continue to do for me. I've finally learned that my life is not my own, but it belongs to you. All I can ask for is that your Will be done in all things and that as hard as you worked to rescue me, you'll be merciful when it comes to my family. I need them and I pray that they see how much they need me. I don't want the need to be for selfish reasons, but because I've missed them and I now know that family is everything when the intent is to succeed in life, love and happiness. Thank you, God, for the opportunity to minister in dance today. I haven't always used my gifts and talents for the upbuilding of your kingdom, but here I am, open to be used by you. I love you, Lord. Amen."

Marissa opened her eyes and what she saw in the mirror was a new woman. She wasn't bitter. She wasn't angry and in the garments of dance used to bless the people of God, she was a blessing not in disguise, but in love.

Coming out of the single dressing room, she joined the other ladies as instructions regarding the holiday program were given out. Standing near the door, she heard a faint knock and turned to open it and joy like she's never felt before came over her. Standing in front of her was the man sent into her life to love her and for her to love.

"You're here!" she exclaimed, stepping out into the hallway and closing the door behind her.

"I know I was running late," Roman said.

"I looked around for you when I first arrived and I didn't see you."

"I just arrived and service is about to start in about ten minutes. You look amazing. Are you first?" he asked.

"No, the full adult ministry is up first, then the children. I'm at the end of service. I do the finale for the play. I'll be sitting in the back most of the service," she explained.

"I'm excited for you and I can't wait to celebrate you. You are so amazing and you look so beautiful. I love you," he blurted out and then stood stoic, hoping his words wouldn't distract her.

"Yyyyou do?" she stammered out.

"I do."

Marissa smiled.

"I love you, too. You made me see what feeling love is supposed to be."

"Because of you, I get to love again," Roman said taking her hands in his. "Can we say a quick prayer?" he asked.

"Yes, of course. There is always room for prayer," she said.

Roman bowed his head as their hands stayed connected.

"Dear Lord, thank you. If I never have another word to utter in your presence, I want to be sure the last words I say are thank you. You've given me so much joy, peace and happiness and for a while, I forgot what those were like and how happy I would be experiencing them again. Today, I want to say a prayer for Marissa that she goes out there and ministers to your glory, finding and receiving love from your people as she does what you have commanded. Thank you for the love we share and we praise you in advance for lives that will be saved today. We're open to your work and we love you, your people and each other. In the name of your son, Jesus, we say, Amen."

When he looked up, Marissa had tears rolling down her face.

"Thank you for that. Can you believe I'm the same person from back in September?" she asked.

"I can because God can do all things. He sent you to help rescue me," he said.

"Isn't that something. I could say the same thing about you. What girl wouldn't want her rescuer to show up looking all dapper in a uniform," she laughed.

"Are you ready?" he asked.

"I am. Do you think they'll show up?" she asked him.

Marissa had been elated to know that he cared about her enough to try and talk to her parents and to also invite them to come and bring Lacey to today's program. Though things had gotten somewhat better and she'd been talking to them and Lacey every day, sometimes twice a day, she wasn't sure if they would come to support her today.

"I don't know, sweetheart, but I'm here and if you need a friendly face, you know where I sit."

"I do."

"Are you going to be okay if your parents don't show up with Lacey?" he asked.

Marissa held her head up high and smiled.

"I will and it's okay. If not today, then another day. I trust God and His will. He's already at work in them because I'm still talking to Lacey every single day and it's been heavenly. Last night, we talked for over an hour and when I saw her yawn, I knew it was time to hang up, but we got a full day's worth of activities talked about in an hour. She also read me a story. Between working the two jobs during the day and classes two nights a week, my life is coming together in a way I never expected."

"I'm happy for you and I'm proud of you. It's all up hill from here. God will always show up when you open yourself to Him. I trusted Him enough to bring you into my life and He's showing He can do pretty good," he smiled.

"I agree. I never thought I could be this happy with someone. You amaze me with how you love and care."

"This is only the beginning, right?" Roman asked.

"Absolutely. I've come to far to turn around now and I like looking into my future and seeing you there. Oh, your mom brought Nina and she's in the children's dressing room putting on her dance outfit. Make sure you clap extra hard for her," she said cheerfully.

"You know I will, just like I will for you. I'm going to get to my seat. I'll see you in the sanctuary," he said and turned and walked away.

Marissa watched Roman walk away and thanked God for the love of a wonderful man. Roman was making a difference in the woman she was because he loved, trusted and supported her along with encouraging her to be her best self.

Going back into the dressing room, she joined the other women as they prepared to minister. Her thoughts turned to her parents and she said a silent prayer that they would come out to support her tonight. She'd given them space and time to figure out if they were ready to work out their problems with her and all she could do was pray and wait and so that's what she's been doing.

**

Marissa listened at the side door to the sanctuary for her cue to come in for her solo performance closing out the holiday play. She still couldn't believe that she'd been asked to do the solo and that the entire women's dance team had been supportive of her. She wasn't sure how she'd be received when they found out she had once been an exotic dance, but none of them looked at her as Delilah. They saw Marissa, a woman who was trying to be closer to God and the life he has for her. She and Raquel even connected again and she apologized for the cold reception she'd been giving her. It turns out, according to Raquel, that she'd always been jealous of her, especially when it came to dance. She had admired Marissa throughout their school years and knew she had what it took to make it big. Raquel complimented her on her ability and Marissa did as any Christian should do and forgave her. Now, they danced together on the same ministry.

Hearing the introduction to her song, she opened the door, held her head up high and trusting God, she walked through the side door and into the sanctuary going straight for the center of the church aisle and took her position. The room was silent until one small voice screamed out at her, startling her.

"Mommy!"

As members of the church began to clap, she looked around trying to find where the voice had come from. She knew that voice and it could only be Lacey.

"Mommy!" she screamed again and this time, she followed the sound of the voice. When her eyes landed on Lacey, she smiled and waved, forgetting for a second that she was in the church. She smiled even brighter when she saw her mother and father waving at her as they sat next to Lacey, smiling with pure joy. God had come through as He said He would and at the point where her life was now, she would never doubt what He could do ever again.

She was about to look away and get back into focus when something caught her eye as she looked into her mother's face. To her, there was a beam of light, like a spotlight that was shining bright right on her parents. For the first time in a long time, she saw a look on her mother's face that wasn't a scowl or a look of disappointment or annoyance. Her mother looked proud and her father looked happy.

"Thank you, God," she said to herself. As Roman

always encouraged her to do, she put her trust in God and He was working it out according to His plan. She blew a kiss to her family and looked to her left where Roman sat along with the other Deacons. Smiling at him, she let her eyes lead his to see her family and he nodded that he'd seen them, too.

Now, she had to focus on the task at hand.

Moving into position, Marissa began to move the moment she heard the first words of Marvin Sapp's hit gospel song, The Best in Me. The song was her personal testimony and was fitting for where she was going through in her own life. When everyone saw the worst in her, God still saw how great she could be. Knowing that had her flying through the air, paying reverence to God and sharing His love through dance with the church.

The song continued and she focused on God, not on the people. She let Him work through her and the people praised. She could hear them shouting and clapping and never in her life would she have dreamed that the applause that meant the most to her would come from the church congregation. Marissa felt like she was floating on air and love blossomed in her – her love for family, her love for Roman, her love for God's people, even her love for Wayne. She no longer held hatred for him in her heart because there wasn't any room with all the love that overflowed from it. Love is what everyone would get from her because God is love.

**

Roman stood clapping like a crazy man along with the rest of the congregation. It finally happened. Marissa allowed God to show up in her and gave Him center stage. She allowed herself to be the vessel to show the people that even someone like her who had been chastised, criticize and crucified could still be the person that God needs to get a message to the people. She had danced beautifully and the glow he saw, not just on her face, by hovering all around her was her not only letting her light shine, but letting others see and feel the power of God at work. As he looked around, some of the women who had been the biggest critics of Marissa when she first came to the church were standing, shouting, crying and thanking God for the ministry of song and dance. He watched as God worked through Deacon Jackie Adams who was shouting and running around the church. He already knew God was going to remove that mean spirit from her. Her reaction was more proof that Marissa was doing the right thing at the right time and at the right place. He searched one of the security guys to come take his place so that he could go and celebrate Marissa as he watched her exit the sanctuary.

As he left the sanctuary, he rushed to the dance room and the moment he arrived, he looked inside and saw her on her knees, praying. Entering the room quietly, he walked over, kneeled with her and placed his hand in hers as he touched and agreed with her prayers of thanks to God for showing her a new day. This was the new start Marissa had been looking for and for him, this new beginning wasn't just for her, but for him, also.

When she finished, she stood and wrapped her arms around him and cried tears of joy. He did what he felt she needed him to do and that was to stand there and allow her to have her moment.

"You were incredible out there tonight. The sanctuary is still on fire from your dance. You looked free. I not only saw it, but I felt it. You're free," he said.

"I feel free. For the first time in my life, I feel free enough to start my life the way I need and want it to be. Thank you for convincing me to come to church. I didn't realize how much I had missed it. Did you see Lacey and my parents?" she asked.

"I did and the whole church heard her cheering on her mommy. She was proud of you and I saw your mother and father. They were proud too, especially your mother," he said.

Marissa stood back when she heard the door open and when she looked in that direction, she saw her mother standing there with tears running down her face. Before Marissa could take a step toward her, Martika rushed into the room and pulled Marissa into her arms and held her tight.

"Mommy!" Marissa cried out in her mother's loving arms once again, a place she had longed to be for so long.

Martika pulled back and held Marissa's tear-stained face in her hands as she spoke directly to her as if they were the only two people in the room.

"I know. It's okay. I'm here and I love you. I'm sorry for everything. I'm sorry for not having a forgiving heart or a loving heart all these years. I was bitter and angry that you didn't live your life the way I wanted, but I know it wasn't up to me to choose how you lived your life. I should have been better support and shown you more love than I did. I should have fought harder for you to see that there was love for you in our home and in our hearts. I'm sorry," she declared.

"I'm sorry too, mommy. Thank you for loving me through it all. I know you did. Thank you for taking care of Lacey and always keeping her love for me alive."

Martika leaned back further and wiped the tears from her own eyes and then those from Marissa's eyes.

"God was at work through you tonight and I was trying to be too stubborn to come. Nothing was going to keep me from it. God said move and I'm learning to be more obedient, even in my old age," she laughed.

"I'm glad," Marissa said laying her head on Martika's chest as her mother's arms once again came around and held her tight.

"I'm going to leave the two of you to some time

alone," Roman said.

Martika waved him over.

"No such thing. Come give me a hug. This man of yours here came by the house and gave your father and me a swift kick in the rear and I want to thank him for loving you as much as he does. Men on the moon can see how much he loves you and that's a good thing," Martika shouted.

"Mommy!"

Marissa turned the moment Lacey came running into the room and into her arms. Hearing her little girl's voice was music to her ears.

"Hi, Pumpkin! I'm so glad you were here tonight for the program," Marissa said with cheer.

"You were really good, mommy. You danced so pretty, mommy. Hi mister Roman," Lacey said turning to him.

"Hello, Lacey. It's good to see you again."

"Is Nina here?" she asked.

"She is. I'll take you to her if your mom and grandma say it's okay," he said looking to them.

Marissa looked at her mother and waited for her to answer.

"Don't look at me, you're her mother. Your father and I are going to head home. Why don't you bring Lacey home later and maybe the two of you can have a sleepover in her room tonight. We would love to have you at home where you belong, Marissa."

"Yippee! Can we? Can you stay the night? Please,

please, please," Lacey pleaded as she bounced around excited.

Marissa began to cry and could barely get her words out.

"Yes, let's have a sleepover. You can ride with me to my place so that I can grab some clothes to sleep in and to wear to work tomorrow. I work here at the church now; did I tell you that? After the work I did with the dance for the children's ministry, I was offered the job of running their new school of dance and helping with teaching some of the dance classes. The church even has a building they purchased that's being renovated. They've asked me to come on board full-time to work in the dance studio. I'll also continue working in the church office, too. I have so much to tell you about tonight!" she exclaimed.

"Oh, Marissa, that's wonderful," Martika said. "I want to hear all about it later. Lacey, go find your friend and make sure you tell Pop-Pop you're staying with your mommy and will be home later. He's still over where we were sitting. He saw some friends he knows," she added.

"I will. I'll be back, mommy. Don't leave without me," she said and waited.

"Never again. Mommy will be right here waiting for you," Marissa said and meant it. No more leaving her baby girl behind. God has a new plan.

Epilogue
Five Months later

Marissa and Roman walked hand in hand through the mall the day before Mother's Day. Nina and Lacey walked ahead of them chattering a mile a minute.

He laughed when he saw a sign for a new movie coming out.

"Look at that?" he said to Marissa and pointed.

They gasped together when they saw the title that said, "coming soon, a new movie, "Rescue Me"".

"That's is crazy!" Marissa said.

"You know we'll have to see that," Roman said.

"It looks like a love story – a chick flick. You're up for that?" she asked.

"Marissa, sweetheart, look at the title. How could I not want to see that? Even if it's not, it's our life story, just in the title alone."

"Yes, it is. You couldn't be righter," she said.

"You know you rescued me, right?" Roman asked as they ordered their ice cream and sat at one table while the girls ate theirs at the table next to them.

"What? I rescued you? How? You were the one who

swooped in at just the right time," she said.

"I was struggling with what to do with myself. I had contemplated leaving the force the very week that I'd met you."

Marissa was surprised.

"You never told me that," she said.

"I know. I didn't feel like I had a purpose anymore when it came to being a cop. Those thoughts were all wrapped up in the guilt I still felt about Melanie, but meeting you that night changed something in me. I didn't know it until later that morning when I saw you. We were meant to meet and fall in love and I do love you. I love you very much," he said.

"I know and I love you, too. I never in a million years thought I would be this in love with anyone. I don't know about rescuing you, but you sure rescued me. That day I was loss too, but for a different reason. You say I rescued you, but you rescued me," she explained.

"We rescued each other and God rescued us both," Roman said.

"I can live with that. Did I tell you about the papers I got earlier today in the mail?"

"How is living with your parents again? Is it still going good?" he asked.

The first week of the new year, Marissa's parents had invited her to move back in with them so that she could be a daily presence in Lacey's life. She didn't hesitate for a minute to accept.

"Wonderful. I can't tell you how happy it makes me to go to bed and wake up to Lacey every single day. The church even allows me time to attend activities at her school during the day."

"Wait, I interrupted your story about papers," he said.

"Wayne signed over all of his rights to Lacey."

"Seriously? Without a fight? I know he never had any interest in being her father, but I assumed out of spite, he would never do that and would have that looming over your head for the rest of your life."

"No fight at all. I'm sure it helped that he'd met you, a man he couldn't swindle or defeat. I went to see him in jail during his trial to talk about Lacey and he said that day when he was arrested, you told him how he messed up coming for me and he said he heard the seriousness in your voice. Most people give into his way of intimidating, but that day he showed up here, you set him straight and that was an awakening for him, too. He knew I wasn't going back to him and he'd never had a connection to Lacey and never wanted one."

"That's amazing. That means when we get married, I can adopt Lacey and you can adopt Nina," Roman said and smiled when Marissa stopped eating her ice cream and let the cone linger in front of her face.

He smiled as he continued eating his as if he didn't just say something to her about marriage.

"I'm sorry, what did you say?" she asked.

"We're going to be sisters!" Lacey screamed.

"Yea!" Nina yelled.

"You heard me. I said when we get married, I can adopt Lacey and you can adopt Nina. We need to be one big family and we don't have to deal with any rights for Wayne."

"We're getting married?" she asked.

"Oh, I plan to propose right, just know that it's coming. I love you, Nina loves you and those two are already sisters according to them. Look at them. When Nina is at home with me, she and Lacey are always on the phone like two old women plotting how to ask us to let them spend the night having a sleepover. I love you so much and I look forward to a happy life of love and family with you. Like I said, I will be asking the right way, so get ready!" he declared.

"And I love you," Marissa said. "Thanks for being exactly what I need."

"It's amazing how God works, isn't it?" he asked.

"I'm glad you had the faith to believe. I didn't come with it, but I have it now, too. God does all things in His own time. I'm glad to be on the receiving end of His goodness."

"Are all still on for dessert after dinner tomorrow?" Roman asked.

"Yes. My mom and dad were excited about finally meeting your parents when I told them you invited us all out for dessert. I'll miss seeing you in church tomorrow since Lacey and I are going with my parents for Mother's Day," she said.

"I know and I'll be waiting to see you later in the day and celebrating."

"This is the best Mother's Day, ever!"

"Yeah, Mommy!" Lacey shouted beside them.

When Roman looked at Nina, he thought he would see sadness as she thought about not having her mother, but she didn't. She looked happily at Marissa."

"If you marry my daddy, then I'm going to have a mommy again, right," she asked.

"Come give me a hug," Marissa said to her.

Roman held back the tears when Marissa picked her up and hugged her tight.

"All this love," Roman said, admiring their affection.

"I know you had a mommy and I'll be your second mommy. I just hope I can do right by your first mommy by being the best second mommy any girl could ever have. We are going to have a wonderful life being mother and daughters, you, me and Lacey."

"I love you, Ms. Marissa," Nina said.

"I love you, too. I love you, too Lacey," she said.

"You are the best mommy! Me and Nina are lucky," Lacey said.

"So is daddy. Now, let's finish our shopping and we can get to our movie," Roman said.

"Yeah! Family time," Nina exclaimed as she and

Lacey stood and started walking ahead of them.

Roman stood, took Marissa hand, pulling her close to him and kissing her sweetly on the lips.

"We're going to be stupid happy!" he uttered against her lips.

"We already are," she replied. "From your lips, to God's ears."

*Enjoy this excerpt from "A Letter to My Mother",
an inspirational novel about forgiveness between
mother and daughter.*

"Hey, Dad, are you here?" Houston hollered as she entered her parents' home. She had an hour left before her shift began at the hospital where she works as a registered nurse. She hated being late, but when her father called saying he needed to talk to her about an urgent matter, she knew nothing could keep her from coming by to see what was going on.

"He'll be right in, Houston," her step-mother Anna said, coming into the room.

"Oh, hi Anna. Do you know what this urgent matter is my dad wants to talk to me about?" she asked.

Houston watched as Anna looked away, not able to look her in the eye. She knew then that Anna knew and she also knew that Anna wouldn't tell her. Whatever it was, it must be serious, she thought.

"Don't quiz your mother when I told you I would tell you when you got here," her father said entering the room.

Nicholas Ray was the greatest man Houston knew and also the best father any girl could have. She turned at the sound of his voice, smiled and ran into his outstretched arms.

"You were sounding all mysterious on the phone and I was anxious to find out what's so important.

You know how you can be all drama-like," she said making fun of the slang her younger twin sisters used.

"I'm going to finish laundry while you two talk," Anna said, in words filled with concern. Houston looked from Anna to her father and noticed he had the same worried look on his face.

"Okay, enough of this, so tell me what's going on," she said, losing patience with not knowing.

As Anna left, Houston joined her father in the sitting room, her favorite place to sit and read as a child growing up.

"Come and sit down Houston," he said, appearing nervous as he clasped his hands together in a manner that let Houston know he had something bad to tell her.

"Just say it since you know I like the bandage on a wound ripped off quickly and not slowly," she said making reference to her desire to always get bad news quick and up front and not have it dragged out.

"Your mother is in a coma in a hospital in California."

Houston was confused considering she'd just seen her mother in the next room. Perhaps her father meant to say another name.

"What are you talking about. Anna seems fine to me."

"Not that mother Houston; I'm talking about your birth mother, Rachel. She's had some kind of accident and is in the hospital and they aren't sure she's going to make it."

Houston stood suddenly, finding it hard to breathe as she tried to wrap her thoughts around his words. She hadn't heard that name in a long time and she'd tried for years to not think about the woman who walked out on her when she was an infant. Her heart began to beat rapidly in her chest at a pace unfamiliar to her. A woman she'd never met, but that she felt close to because her blood ran through her very own veins, was dying before she'd ever been able to set eyes on her.

"Houston, are you okay? Take your time and ask me whatever you need to," she heard her father say calmly.

She paced trying to gather her thoughts, not knowing where to begin with her questions. There was much she wanted to know.

Through the years her father tried to answer questions about her mother, but she knew he was holding back, not wanting to tarnish the memory of her mother for her. He'd always told her that it wasn't his place to tell her mother's story and that he hoped one day Rachel would tell her own story to Houston, but that day never came and Houston had resolved that she would never get to meet the woman who gave her life.

She turned back to her father, not just to ask questions, but for the comfort she knew she'd find by looking into his face.

"What happened to her?" she asked coming back to sit next to him.

"I don't know all of the details other than she was in a car accident and that her injuries are pretty severe. She slipped into a coma a few days ago, and they aren't offering her family much hope."

Houston's radar went up when she heard her father say the word, 'family'.

"What family? You've always said she didn't have any family?"

Houston remembered her father telling her when he'd met Rachel many years ago, that she was living with a foster family and that she had no biological family that he knew of.

Her father continued on.

"The family I'm speaking of is her husband, Marcus Ealy and her son Mark."

Houston's reaction to hearing that Rachel had a son showed on her face in a way that put her father's guard up.

"Her name is Rachel Ealy and she's been alive all this time with a husband and a son?" she asked.

"Houston, before you fly off the handle, yes Rachel has a husband and son and until her accident, she was well and living in California. Her son is in his twenties and in the Navy and I knew nothing about him or her husband until yesterday. Let me try to explain as much as I can about what I know based on what I was told."

Houston knew to calm herself down and not get angry or even feel jealous about the fact that a woman who didn't want her desired and had another child, one who got to grow up with her.

"Rachel must have known where we were, but for how long I don't know. Her best friend Lana came to see me at the office yesterday and at the time, I thought she was a new client when she asked to speak to me. I sat in my office while she explained to me who she was. I should have recognized her since she's an actress. She told me about the accident and that Rachel has been living in California for some years now after spending some time overseas with her husband who recently retired from the military. They made their home in California some years ago. She also mentioned that she was able to locate me because Rachel told her who I was and had also told her about you. She didn't go into detail about how much she knew about you, but she didn't want Rachel to pass away and you not know that she was still alive all this time."

Houston shook her head, not believing that her father was telling her that Rachel was alive all these years, obviously knew where they were and made no effort to contact them.

"I can't believe she's been alive this whole time."

"I know this comes as a shock Houston. Lana told me that the accident happened about a week ago. She's apparently in really bad shape. From what I understand, her husband has agreed to a date of when he will allow them to remove her from life support. Lana told him that she wanted to reach out to you to see if you wanted to fly out to California and then he would make the decision on the date. There is no pressure here for you to do anything and whatever you decide to do, I'm in full support of it. Houston, I know you don't know her and there were a lot of years of hurt that you and I had to work through, so you think on this and if you want to go, I'll go with you, stand with you and comfort you in any way you need. If you decide you don't want to do anything at all, I will respect and support that too."

Nicholas Ray waited, practically holding his breath waiting on his daughter to take it all in. He knew it was painful for her to hear that Rachel had been alive for the past thirty years, all of Houston's life, and had not once tried to reach out and contact them. He didn't care how long it took, he would sit and remain quiet until she let him know how he could help her through this.

"Daddy she could die and it would be life as usual for me since it's like she's been dead for the past thirty years anyway."

She looked to him for support in the way she was feeling.

"Does that sound too harsh or even morbid? I don't want it to sound that way. I don't know how to react to this. My first thought is to not go and feel the hurt all over again of her being snatched from my life as if she's walking away again. My second thought is, though she is in a coma, I would like to see her before she passes away. I don't know if I would have anything to say, but I'd like the goodbye to be on my terms and not hers like it was thirty years ago. I want to know what you think about what I should do."

Houston grasped her father's hands and as they looked at each other for comfort, she knew that he would give her his honest opinion without judgement.

"It doesn't sound harsh or even morbid for you to feel that way. Your feelings about Rachel are yours. If for no other reason than to look upon her and have the chance to say goodbye, which is something you have been unable to do all these years, I say do it. If this is all you get of Rachel, then this will be all that you will need. God allowed Lana to reach out to me yesterday when I know that she could have let Rachel slip away and die and never tell us about it. This could be exactly what you need to finally get closure, though it's not the closure you'd want. We do have one thing that we have to consider and that is, I don't know the date that her husband will choose to have her removed from life support and your wedding is coming up in a month. I don't want this to put a damper on your special day. I've been looking forward to walking you down the aisle to give you away to Noah. This shouldn't be a cloud over that day."

Houston was set to marry the love of her life, Noah

in just over thirty days. She needed to talk to Noah because her mind was made up.

"I know and I need to talk to Noah about all this since it impacts him too. There's a lot to think about and still a lot to do for the wedding."

Her father shook his head in agreement with her.

"Yes, there is. I have a phone number for Lana if you would like to get the latest on Rachel's condition. I told her I would either let her know myself or have you call her with your plans. What are you thinking about doing?" he asked.

Houston thought about what he'd said and agreed that the little bit of closure she could get from this would-be worth the lifetime of hurt and pain she'd always felt, not knowing why her mother never wanted her.

"I'm going to go see her to say my goodbye. I only have one more week of work before taking the next two months off for the wedding, honeymoon and moving out of my condo and into our new home. I'm going to ask if I can take the extra week and go as soon as possible after I've discussed this with Noah. I'll give Lana a call today to see if the family has made any decisions about life support. I want to get there before they do."

This wasn't the conversation she wanted to eventually have with her father about her birth mother, but she was thankful that he told her. Lana didn't have to come all this way to tell him about

Rachel and he didn't have to tell her. He could have let her live her life never knowing, especially if Rachel passed away. As far as she was concerned, in her mind, Rachel had died years ago. That thought gave her comfort instead of the other option which was that Rachel was happily living a life and never thought about the daughter she left behind.

"Thank you, Daddy, for loving me so much. I know hearing that Rachel has been alive all these years is as much a shock for you as it is for me. She left us thirty years ago and never looked back. I don't know why, but I'm hoping to get some peace and understanding from my visit to see her. I know you want to be there with me and for me through all of this, but I want to go alone. I have so much I want to think about and I'd like to take some time for reflection. I may stay more than one day and Anna and my sisters need you here. I promise I will call you often and anytime you want to check on me, I will have my phone on day and night. Let me talk to Lana and Noah and then I'll let you know my plans. I hope you're okay with that."

Houston wanted to tread lightly and didn't want her father's feelings hurt knowing that even after all these years and the good life and unconditional love that he and Anna have given her, that she still longed to see Rachel.

"I'm following your lead on this and I will be here in any capacity that you need. Promise me that before you board a plane going anywhere, that you will take some time and pray about forgiveness. I've told you many times in the past that even though I was hurt when she left us, I forgave her a long time ago because you can't live a life consumed with hate for someone because they didn't choose the life you wanted them to choose. Whatever Rachel's reasons were, they were her reasons and though I know you missed having a mother in your life before I married Anna, God has blessed your life tremendously. Pray for clarity and understanding and don't question why God has made the decision to call Rachel home before you can have a chance to have her as a part of your life. Know that He is responsible for granting you this little time with Rachel, so make it count. I love you and day or night, you pick up that phone if you need to hear my voice and if you need me there, I'll be on the first flight out."

Houston nodded her head as a few tears fell to her cheek. She loved her father and was thankful that he had always been there for her, never giving up on her.

"Thank you, Daddy, and because I've watched you live your life without regret, without hatred or anger over Rachel, I promise you I will pray about forgiveness and understanding. Thank you for showing me early in my life who God is and because of that, I know I can make it through this and will be able to walk away without any hatred in my heart. I believe I need to do this in order to finally put closure to the unknown even if it's just to see her and not hear from her."

She stood to leave and as her father stood, she hugged him with a tight bear hug. He has always put her first, took care of her and never gave her reason to doubt that he loved her more than anything. They've always had a special bond and because of that, she knew he would help see her through this.

"I love you Dad."

"I love you, too, Houston. You have always been that breath of fresh air that makes everything in my life worth living. I'm proud of you and we will both make it through this. I'll tell your sisters you were here since they're still in school."

"Tell them I'll call them later. I want to know what they think of their dresses for the wedding. They had final fittings yesterday and they looked gorgeous. I'll go give Anna a hug before I leave. I know I don't have to tell her, but I want her to know how much I love her, especially with all of this with Rachel. Nothing and no one could ever take her place in my life as the mother who gives me love and support. She stepped into her role as my mother and I'm thankful for her."

Get "A Letter to my Mother" in paperback and download from www.cherylbarton.net or www.crbarton.comtext here.

More Inspirational Novels

One Sister Away: Encouraging Words from One Sister to Another, Volumes 1 – 4

One Sister Away is a compilation project birthed from the heart and spirit of Author Cheryl Barton, bringing together sisters from all walks of life to inspire and encourage another sister. One Sister Away is filled with poetry, short stories, testimonies and short passages of encouragement that will have all readers proclaiming, "I Am My Sister's Keeper." We, as sisters, are more powerful when we come together than we are apart. Be blessed by our words.

Get all four volumes
https://www.crbarton.com/one-sister-away-series

About the Author

Cheryl Barton lives in Maryland and in her spare time she loves to read espionage, crime and romance novels, cook, watch Sci-fi movies, spend time with family and friends and enjoy Maryland steamed crabs. Cheryl is celebrating 30 years as a government employee and loves writing romance novels when she's not working. Cheryl is the author of 31 romance novels, 3 inspirational novels and is proud of 4 book compilation projects with several other incredible women called, "One Sister Away: Encouraging Words from One Sister to Another" – a series of books meant to encourage, empower and inspire other women. People often ask Cheryl which book is her favorite of all of those she's written. While she finds it hard to select one favorite, Cheryl still looks to her first novel, Bachelor Not for Sale, if she had to pick a favorite because it was her first novel and the one that inspired her to continue writing.

Cheryl was a 2018 Finalist of the Literary Trailblazer of the Year award, given by the Indie Author Legacy Awards' yearly event. Cheryl is a member of the Romance Writers of America – National Chapter and the Maryland Romance Writers. She is also a member of the Black Writers' Guild of Maryland and a member of the International Women Writers Guild.

Indulge in more romance and inspirational novels by visiting her website at www.cherylbarton.net.

About the Publisher

Cheryl Barton Publishing, LLC, a subsidiary of Cheryl Barton Productions, is a book publishing company based out of Maryland. Our foundation is based on the belief that there is a writer in all of us, so just do it! Let us help you get moving toward that dream today!

Our company motto is, "Your Dreams Are Safe in Our Hands" and we stand behind that.

For more information on the services provided by Cheryl Barton Publishing, LLC and to see other book selections, visit our website at www.crbarton.com

Authors at Cheryl Barton Publishing, LLC
www.crbarton.com

Keep it Simple & Sexy
by Lafon F. Porter

Ponder This: Just a Bit of Inspiration
P.S. Still Pondering
by JoAnn Wilson

Maximize Moments: 40 Day Devotional,
Volume 2
by Dr. Lisa Weah

The Wake
by Kyle Berkley